Alan looked inquiringly over Stephen's shoulder, into the dark tunnels of the bush behind him. "Where's Cherry?"

"Following along," Stephen replied. He turned, expecting to see Cherry appearing between the trees.

In the momentary silence, the two men realized the bush was silent. No one was approaching.

"Where's Cherry?" Alan demanded. "Damn it, man, have you left her behind in that bloody jungle?"

NOBODY READS JUST *ONE* LUCY WALKER!

Available in Beagle editions

If not available at your dealer, they may be ordered by mail. Send 80¢ for each book (includes postage and handling charges) to Beagle Books, Dept. CS, 36 West 20 Street, New York, N.Y. 10011. Please note that not all books may be available at all times.

THE CALL OF THE PINES

Lucy Walker

BEAGLE BOOKS • NEW YORK

Published by arrangement with Crown Publishers, Inc.

First printing: December 1970
Second printing: April 1971
Third printing: May 1972
Fourth printing: June 1973

Printed in the United States of America

BEAGLE BOOKS, INC.
201 East 50 Street, New York, NY 10022

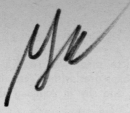

CHAPTER ONE

Cherry lay in her bed in the bright early morning of her nineteenth birthday and watched the light filtering through the muslin curtains of her bedroom.

It was a lovely bedroom, a lovely summer morning, and Cherry, without knowing it, was a delightful girl. No one could say she had any claims to real beauty yet her dark hair, now spread on the white pillow, her smooth sun-tanned skin, her dark blue eyes and mobile mouth were very attractive. More than this there was a touch of ingenuous charm of which she was quite unconscious. She was a mixture of the old world and the modern and at the moment hadn't discovered for herself to which world she belonged.

To-day was even more momentous than being a birthday. It was the end of a long road, for Cherry had a week ago received her certificate at the Kindergarten Training College.

It was like being at the top of a hill. It all looked so simple, that clear view of her future life. Already she had been offered a post in her old school. Cherry's parents had wondered if it was wise to take this post. Wouldn't it be better, they had suggested, to try something different at first? After all, Cherry's life had been very limited up to date.

There were reasons for this deep thoughtfulness on the part of the Landins.

Cherry was not their own child, in the sense that she had not been born to them. She had come to them, a treasure eagerly sought, as a newborn child, at the time of her own mother's death. Her father had been killed in the Korean war.

Mrs. Landin had taken the child with almost frightened eagerness and brought her up as her own.

In plain fact the Landins had so eagerly wanted a child

5

and Cherry coming to them was such a joy, they had, they now feared, perhaps overlavished care and guardianship. Cherry was so quiet and shy in company they now feared for her.

The walls of her room had been painted a soft grey and the ceiling a gay pink. There was a modern bed with an inner spring mattress and cupboards and a table that matched the bed's honey-coloured woodwork. Curtains and cushions consorted across the room with one another in a gay floral pattern, and there was a little chair with curved legs, and her own books and pictures. On the mantelshelf, polished and shining, was her collection of china ornaments and figurines.

Cherry had woken so early she had lain in bed in this delightful room listening to the murmuring sound of the sea which lay at the foot of the Street of the Pines, not two hundred yards away. She didn't have to go to the window to know what the sea would look like this early summer morning. It would be a brilliant blue and beyond it on the horizon would be the islands. The water would be placid and the early swimmers would already be dotting the curved edges of the shining yellow beach.

For three week-ends now, after Cherry had run down the Street of the Pines to the beach for her early morning dip, she had been aware of a tall man, bronzed not only by the seaside but only too obviously by a life in the outback, sitting on the sands near the water's edge.

He wore black bathing trunks and his rubber sandals lay with his towel on the sand beside him. He always sat the same way, his knees drawn up, his elbows resting on them. He sat and smoked a cigarette, watching the other swimmers.

Evidently he liked to swim early and thereafter liked to sun-bake.

Cherry had a curious feeling that he watched her, but not more than he watched others. She had a feeling she would like to see him stand up, run across that sand, and dive into the water as everyone else did. She was always either too late or too early for this activity. He did swim,

6

of that she was assured, for his hair, dark and tousled, was sometimes wet, and if she passed near enough she could see the salt and wet sand glistening on his powerful brown arms.

It had been some time after Cherry had first noticed this tall man sun-baking on the sands that she realised he was living in the house on the other side of the Street of the Pines. This house, a broad-fronted bungalow, had had a *For Sale* notice nailed to the fence for some time. Then the notice disappeared and in its place came painters with their ladders and general paraphernalia. The house must have been bought and now it was being done up.

Mr. and Mrs. Landin did not evince very much interest in the goings-on at the house across the street. In the first place it was a very wide street with verges on either side. The pines, tall and old, musical in the wind, grew right down the centre of the street as well as a chain and a half away on each side. It wasn't one street, it was two streets lying side by side and what went on beyond the centre pines was quite a long way away. Moreover, the Landins, being politely brought up and " old-fashioned," would not dream of inquiring into other people's business.

Cherry might have cast surreptitious glances at the new house emerging from the old one as a result of some considerable face-lifting, but like her parents, she wouldn't have presumed to be overtly curious.

She could not help noticing the fluttering of life in that house when the painters and renovators had gone. There had been a big overlanding car with a country number turning in at the drive gates. The middle-aged woman who arrived daily at eight in the morning and left at five in the evening was quite evidently a domestic help of some kind.

Except that Cherry knew that someone quite different from the former owners lived there now she had not continued to probe.

One morning she had been walking up the sloping street from the beach when one of her College friends offered her a lift home. It was only two hundred yards to her home but Cherry accepted the offer because she liked her friend and it was pleasant to be with her for a few minutes. The car passed along the left-hand side of the centre pines, on what was called the "down road" and it pulled up opposite Cherry's home and right outside the newly-painted house.

It was then that Cherry saw the tall man of the beach. He was emerging through the gate, wearing black swimming trunks and with a towel slung round his shoulders.

Cherry flushed because she hadn't known herself she was so curious about this man.

"Yes," was her immediate thought, "he is tall! Taller than Dad . . . taller than anyone I know. And he lives *there*. How strange I didn't know!"

Cherry was much too shy to glance again in the direction of the tall man. She looked quickly away, embarrassed at her own interest.

Not so her friend, who *whistled*.

"Phew, phew! Nice neighbours you have round here, Cherry. What's his name?"

"I haven't any idea. I didn't even know he lived there."

Her friend looked at her pityingly.

"You do miss some fun, don't you, Cherry? If I lived where you live and he lived where he lives I'd not only know his name but I'd know what he does and if he's married."

"But I'm not you," said Cherry lamely; though for a minute she wished she were.

Now she knew four things about him. He went swimming more than once a day so it didn't look as if he worked at anything, unless he was just living in that house on holiday. The big car she had seen going into the driveway carried a country number. Probably he was someone down from the outback on holiday. It accounted for that deeply bronzed skin, the small lines around his dark grey eyes.

Yes, she had garnered four things about him and it was like a little secret treasure heap. He was tall, really tall, and he went swimming more than once a day. He came from the country and he lived in the house across the street.

Cherry, lying in her bed in the early morning of her

8

nineteenth birthday, thought about the beach and the ocean lying out there at the foot of the street. Thinking about it she saw it in her imagination, not as it really was at this early hour, but as it would be three hours hence with the tall man sitting on the sands, his knees drawn up under him. He would be holding a cigarette in his hand and his black hair would be tousled and wet and the salt and sand would be shining on his arms and shoulders.

All the time Cherry, lying in her bed, had been thinking this dream she had heard in the background the sound of the rattle of teacups, the throb of the hot water jug coming to the boil, the soft movements of her mother in the kitchen. In a minute there would be a tap on the door and the early morning birthday cup of tea. It would be on a small round tray and beside the teacup would be a plate with wafer-thin bread and butter on it. Beside the plate would be the birthday present.

True to tradition there came, presently, that tap on the door and Mrs. Landin came in.

She was a small quiet woman with her greying hair drawn back in an old-fashioned bun at the back of her head. She wore rimless glasses which never hid the kindly expression in her long-sighted eyes.

This morning her smile was tinged with anxiousness for she had something more to offer Cherry than morning tea in bed and a small square parcel which at the moment concealed a charming marcasite bracelet. *To go with your watch, dear,* as she later explained.

She kissed Cherry and said what a lovely day it was and after the present had been opened and examined and exclaimed over, she sat on the foot of her daughter's bed.

Now the anxiety came more clearly to the surface for Mrs. Landin had something to say and she was very anxious to say it all the right way.

"Darling," she said, "Dad and I've been talking about you – now you've finished College. We've been plotting, I'm afraid. We've been making plans."

Her voice faltered and Cherry felt a faint constriction

9

of the heart as she sipped her tea and watched her mother. Intuitively she knew something momentous was coming. Mrs. Landin, who never fidgeted as a principle, was now toying with the pattern on Cherry's pretty candlewick bedcover. Gradually the story of the plotting and planning came out.

Cherry's own natural father had been head stockman on a cattle station in the far north before he had gone to the Korean war and been killed. Vaguely, Mr. and Mrs. Landin, who were anxious for Cherry to go out into the world and try her own feet, had guessed Cherry's unspoken interest in the things of the far north. She should go there, they thought. She should go and visit the place where she had been born. Everyone, Mrs. Landin explained, had a feeling for the place from which they came. That was their own piece of earth.

Seeing the silent surprise on Cherry's face when Mrs. Landin got this far, the story was nervously hurried on.

"You don't have to go if you don't want to, darling. Not for the world would we insist. But we think it a good thing. So we got a job for you up there. Now, it's all out! Yes, a job. On a station. You don't have to go, and of course the people haven't seen you yet so they might change their minds too. But if you'd like to go we'd like you to go. Just for a year. After that you can come back and . . . and . . . well, kindergarten teach at your old school, if there's a vacancy."

Cherry was so surprised she couldn't say anything for a moment. She didn't know whether or not this surprise was so big it was a shock. It was nearly a minute before she could find her voice and in any event she had to swallow a piece of bread and butter first.

"But, Mother, what kind of a job?"

She couldn't say she didn't want to go away — that suddenly a dream of a beach with a tall man sitting on it for ever and ever had been shattered — that suddenly the security and foundation of her home had moved an inch under her as if warning her that nothing stays the same for ever.

Perhaps they wanted . . . perhaps they thought . . . No,

no! It couldn't be that. They couldn't possibly feel they had finished with her and that they had done everything they could do for this child who was not born their own and that they were now ejecting her gently and kindly but remorselessly from the nest.

Cherry swallowed the thought with her bread and butter. It couldn't be!

"What . . . what sort of a job?" she asked helplessly.

"A governess, dear. You'd like that, wouldn't you? It's the same as teaching. It's a little girl on Yulinga Station in the north. There's a small baby too only you wouldn't have to teach him. Only the little girl. They want someone to break her in for school next year."

Mrs. Landin looked at her daughter with all her anxiety shining from behind the spectacles. Her hand had stopped tracing the pattern on the candlewick bedcover.

Cherry leaned back against her pillow and closed her eyes momentarily.

Now she had to be careful. How often in the daily round did the adopted child have to be careful – and the adopted parents be doubly careful? Always everybody was trying to do what true daughters and true parents would do, but never quite succeeding.

A real daughter would say . . . "Oh, Mummy, you do talk rot. Besides, I want to find my own jobs."

Cherry couldn't say that. She had to know first why Dad and Mum had made all these plans without telling her. She mustn't hurt their feelings. In the last analysis she might have to do as they asked, rather than have them think she was anything but a loving and real daughter. To go north? Yes, that was an adventure. A month ago it would have seemed wonderful.

She opened her eyes.

"Yes," she said. "Governessing would be nice. What sort of a station is it, Mummy?"

"Yulinga Station. A beautiful one, I believe. Of course I know there are some wretched ones and there are also some very grand ones. This one is very good, they say.

Very, very good. They have everything modern. You know, hot water systems and refrigeration and a garden. They even have the cinema there for their stockmen. I saw some photographs of it."

" How did you find out about it?" Cherry asked, trying desperately to sound eager.

" At the pastoral agency. We saw the advertisement in the paper and Dad went in. They said a member of the family would be down in town for a few weeks at Christmas and would interview you. And darling, he's here. No, we haven't seen him yet. We're to make an appointment——"

Cherry tried to think and look interested at the same time.

What was behind this? Were the darlings just being old-fashioned again, thinking they must do everything, but *everything,* for their helpless daughter? Was this merely misguided kindness, or had her days of home and security ended? Was this what being adopted meant? Two nice people took in a baby and brought her up, then, hey presto! Their job was done. Out into the world!

Cherry, whose eyes had closed again, opened them and looked down the length of the bed at her mother's face. There she read so much kindness as well as nervous anxiety she could not bring herself to believe this.

" Mother," she said, " that was wonderful of you and Dad to go to so much trouble. I think perhaps I ought to see this person who has come down from the station. But what . . . what . . ." she faltered.

She had been going to say, " What if I don't like this person? What if I don't like the job they offer me?" Instead she finished her sentence somewhat lamely—" What if they don't like me? And I don't suit?"

" Oh, you will, dear. I'm certain of it. They haven't anyone else applying and you've got such a good report from school, as well as your College certificate."

Mrs. Landin suddenly looked a little prim.

" And you come from a nice home and have been correctly brought up. That counts, you know. It's very important their little daughter should be taught good manners."

Cherry laughed.

"I don't know, Mother," she said as she threw aside the bedcovers and sprang out of bed. Her pretty sprigged muslin pyjamas were lovely but she had never had the heart to tell her mother they should have been "shortie" pyjamas. Long ones were "out" as far as the young people of to-day were concerned. Anyhow she liked her pyjamas. She was glad she was not as bullying as her friends who just wouldn't wear what their mothers bought for them, if they weren't the very last thing in teenager wear.

"Heaven only knows what people want their children taught these days. Manners change and get out of date so quickly," Cherry said.

"Never!" said Mrs. Landin, rising from the foot of the bed. "A well-bred woman is the end result of a well-bred child. I'm sure you learned that much in your Kindergarten College."

"We learned about freedom and the 'play way' of learning. I think everyone's a bit bewildered about the end result nowadays."

Mrs. Landin went to the door.

"I expect you want to go down for your swim after breakfast, dear," she said. "Don't forget to let Dad be awfully surprised it's your birthday, will you? We mustn't spoil his fun."

"I won't," promised Cherry to this last request.

CHAPTER TWO

True to form Dad looked astounded that another birthday had come around. As he had done since Cherry was fifteen, he rooted round in his pocket for something new and something blue. The blue five pound note could not be found. Instead there was a beautiful, crinkly, brown ten-pound note.

"Must have forgotten to change it yesterday," he said. "Ah well, you're grown up now, Cherry. I guess a ten-pound note is more appropriate. At least it's new. What a piece of luck I had it with me."

It was then he dropped a millstone into the domestic pond.

" There's a gentleman residing in the house over the street. He's calling to see you at noon to-day. Did Mother tell you all about it? Believe it or not, he wants to take you up north to live on his station for a year. There's a small girl wants some teaching. And up there, on that station, they've actually heard of you. How's that, Cherry girl, for a start out in life?"

" Oh, Dad!"

Cherry wanted to laugh and cry at the naïveté of this grey-haired man with the twinkling eyes, at the foot of the table.

" As if he'd heard of me without you and Mother having something to say about it."

She stopped short.

A man living in a house across the street.

She put down the spoon with which she had been dipping into the iced grapefruit.

"Which house do you mean, Dad?" she asked, trying to make her voice sound natural.

" The one that was for sale. You might have noticed it has been renovated. Some people called Denton from Yulinga Station have bought it as their town house. Mr. Stephen Denton is down from the north to set it in order and have something of a holiday, too, I think." Mr. Landin now looked as near mischievous as a man of his age could do. " He is the member of the family who is to interview the new governess."

Cherry returned his smile weakly. She picked up her spoon and dipped it into the grapefruit again.

"What is he like?" she asked without looking up. " I mean what does he look like?"

" I've no idea. I haven't met him. All our negotiations have been through the pastoral company."

Cherry had a fleeting mental picture of the tall man sitting on the sand with his knees drawn up under him.

Could it be? *Could* it be?

14

But of course it was. There was only one man living in that house. Cherry was sure of it. Now she knew he was married, and had a little girl of eight as well as a young baby. That was why he sat alone and did not make himself friendly with other people on the beach. His heart was in the north-west with his wife and children.

Cherry's heart sank, not because she was disappointed that a dream had vanished like the mirage that so often lay around the islands out to sea, but because she would now have to go through the ordeal of being interviewed by someone she had seen almost daily and with whom she had never spoken.

Did one confess to having seen him or did one pass everything off as if he were an absolute stranger?

Oh, this was too difficult! How could Mother and Dad be so other-worldly they didn't know that girls of nineteen were adult and had minds of their own, and ambitions of their own.

Cherry raised hurt eyes.

"Dad," she said out of her hurt, "I believe you want me to go away. I don't think you want me any more."

There was a painful silence round the breakfast table as Mr. and Mrs. Landin looked at their daughter and saw the scarcely veiled anxiety, even accusation, in her eyes. This was something for which they had not bargained.

Mr. Landin put down the napkin with which he was at that moment wiping his mouth.

"Cherry," he said, "don't ever say that again. Not as long as you live. You belong to us and what is much more important we belong to you."

"I'm sorry I said that, Dad. It was just the embarrassment of meeting that man. I suppose it is always easier to run away from an awkward situation."

"Darling," said Mrs. Landin hurriedly, "you don't have to go. I mean, it was only an idea. You see . . ."

"It's all right, Mother," said Cherry. "Of course I'd like to go. That is if they will have me. It's only that I've never been away before; and I'm – well, I'm nervous about being interviewed. I said the first thing that came into my head."

"Next time have a second thought before you speak, Cherry," Mr. Landin said, rising from his seat. He turned away and went to the door, then he looked back. "You are nineteen and adult," he said slowly. "You have to find out how the world ticks while you're young and resilient. I think you should go away for a year, but if the idea of Yulinga does not appeal then we must think of something else."

He stood framed in the doorway as he felt in his pocket for his pipe. Slowly he filled it and packed it. During this process neither Mrs. Landin nor Cherry stirred.

He lifted his head and looked at Cherry across the room.

"One year will be a long time for us, Cherry. We'll live through it. However, if you promise to come back to us then. . . ."

"Oh, Dad . . ." cried Cherry, pushing back her chair and rising. She ran across the room and caught his sleeve as he turned to go through the door.

He patted her hand but went on through the door and down the passage without saying anything more.

Cherry followed his spare figure with her eyes. She knew that she had hurt him in some unforgivable way but she knew too that she would make it up to him. She would come back to him. Wherever she was in the world she would come home again.

As she turned round to face her mother she determined that she would meet the man from across the street, and in some intangible way it would be a different Cherry from the inexperienced young girl who had run down to the beach each morning with her head full of vapid dreams about a man whose very name she did not know.

It would be Cherry Landin, the governess-elect, who would meet Mr. Stephen Denton at noon on this bright summer day.

It was three minutes after noon when Stephen Denton strolled across the double way of the Street of the Pines.

Cherry had not gone for her swim this morning. It would be too much to bear, she thought, to see him without being acknowledged, or for that matter acknowledging him, and then meet him as a prospective employer an hour or two later.

She had lightly made the excuse of wanting to be at home on her birthday morning.

"Besides," she added as she helped in the kitchen with the dishes, " I don't want to be all fussed up when that man from Yulinga Station comes."

Subtly, the tall mystery man of the beach had become now "that man from Yulinga."

Cherry didn't like him any more though she hadn't the faintest idea why there had been this change of heart. It had something to do with a soap-bubble that had burst, but Cherry told herself he was just an aloof rich man who had taken no interest in his neighbours. She quite ignored the fact that his neighbours had taken no interest in him.

None of this was quite logical but then Cherry was far from being in a logical mood this morning. A soap-bubble had burst so she was disappointed and missed the iridescent radiance upon which she had been dreaming.

He came across the street, dressed in a dark-blue reefer jacket, his deep-grey trousers impeccably pressed and a spotted stock tucked in the open neck of his white shirt. His hair was combed down flat across his head. Cherry could look directly into his face now, as Mrs. Landin brought him into the sitting-room and made the introductions.

He had a square brow and a straight nose. His eyebrows were very dark and strongly marked and under them his eyes, a dark grey, looked at Cherry keenly, and then politely looked away to Mrs. Landin.

Yes, he was very tall. Six feet two, at least, Cherry thought. His shoulders were broad and he moved with the ease and precision of an athlete. At close quarters he had the unmistakable look of the north-west pastoralist, the type that was sunburnt, had good strong hands, a slow deliberate way of speaking, yet somehow managed to convey a capacity

17

for speed in movement if necessary. Above everything else he looked like a man with a will of his own and one who made up his own mind quickly and silently and went his own way.

Mrs. Landin introduced Cherry to him and there was a sudden flashing puckish smile that lit up his whole face, and made Cherry's heart quiver a little.

" How do you do?" he said. His voice was quiet and firm.

" Very nice," Cherry thought sadly, and wondered why she was sad.

It was a curious feeling, standing there acknowledging the greeting of a man who was about to add, subtract, divide and multiply the facets of her own personality in order to decide whether he would have her to guide and teach his own child. Specially as, after that one illuminating smile, he turned and paid attention to Mrs. Landin, and not herself.

Mrs. Landin asked him to sit down and then they all three sat in something like a semicircle round the small room. Cherry, her hands in her lap, her feet neatly crossed at the ankles, was opposite Stephen Denton but she saw only his profile as he listened to Mrs. Landin politely, without interruption, as she eagerly and with some over-emphasis set about praising Cherry. It was a very good profile.

" How dear and quaint Mother is," Cherry thought a little ruefully. " As if he could possibly be interested in what I looked like as a child, and how many people had said I was a very nice girl. In a minute – oh, awful thought – Mummy will bring out photographs."

She also thought how desperately embarrassed she would have been if somehow everything had not changed since the morning and she had learned he was a married man. Why hadn't she guessed before? She would have spared herself all that foolish daydreaming.

She also felt a certain wry amusement at the picture of early Victorian girlhood she must look in reality, as well as in the legend that her mother was now developing breathlessly.

She was sitting straight-backed in her upright chair as

befitted an applicant for the post of governess. She was unaware that her pale primrose summer dress set off her oval face and the dark hair that didn't quite do as it was told, her long sun-tanned arms and her slender youthful figure.

But then, Mr. Denton of Yulinga Station was not inclined to look at her anyway.

"Cherry loves children and she would like to go to the north-west because, you see, she was born there. But of course she doesn't remember it. She was only two weeks old when she was brought down here——"

Stephen Denton turned his head and glanced at Cherry. There must have been something that amused him for Cherry distinctly saw a fleeting smile in his eyes, and the corners of his mouth drew in. There was nothing amusing about herself, Cherry thought, so he must be laughing at Mummy.

Of course he would laugh at Mummy. He should understand that though Mummy was old-fashioned and was doing all the talking, when Cherry as the applicant should have been doing it, she had a heart of pure gold and no one, but *no one*, was permitted to laugh at her.

Cherry was torn between giving Mr. Denton a haughty look, and remaining demure, as befitted an applicant for a post. She decided on demureness for her mother's sake, and not that of the tall handsome prospective employer.

Her mother was going on and on about Cherry as a girl, Cherry as a student, Cherry as a daughter about the house. Mrs. Landin thought she was drawing a lovely picture of her beloved daughter but Cherry knew it was a silly one. In a minute Stephen Denton would ask why she, Cherry, didn't speak up for herself.

"So you see, your little girl will be in the safest hands . . ." Mrs. Landin was saying triumphantly. "What do you call your daughter, Mr. Denton?"

"The little girl in question is called Sandra, Mrs. Landin. But she's not my daughter. She is my brother's daughter. They have a twelve-months-old baby too. A boy——"

"Then you're not married?" asked Mrs. Landin. She

looked perplexed. Cherry knew just what had sprung into her mother's mind now. If he wasn't married then what sort of a judge could he be as to who was fit to undertake the teaching of a child? Mother did not believe in bachelors, any more than young spinsters, knowing anything about the facts of life at all. Inside herself, suddenly and foolishly, there was a new moonrise for a daydream.

"I'm afraid not," said Stephen Denton. Once again he glanced round but turned his face quickly back to Mrs. Landin. "I could rectify that state of affairs any moment, you know, if you think it's necessary to qualify me to take your daughter back to Yulinga with me."

Now he did smile and even Mrs. Landin knew he was making mild fun at her expense.

"Oh, it isn't that," Mrs. Landin said hastily. "I was thinking your brother, and his wife, must have great faith in your judgment. And Cherry – you see, well, Cherry will not have met them."

"In that case she will have to take the same chance on them as they will take on her," he said firmly. Cherry wasn't sure whether he was making fun this time or not. Neither was Mrs. Landin. In fact he was not making fun.

Yet his words implied that Cherry would have the job. How could he tell what she was like? Except for saying "How do you do" when he came in Cherry had not uttered a word.

"May I smoke?" he asked Mrs. Landin politely. He reached in his pocket for his cigarettes and his matches.

"Oh, of course. Please do." Mrs. Landin hastily took an ash-tray, never before used as anything but an ornament, from the top of the television set. Cherry knew she should have performed that small service instead of her mother. Somehow she was glued to her chair by the fact she did not want to do anything for Stephen Denton; she was certain he had been quietly laughing at her mother.

Instead it was he who stood up. He took several steps across the room, offered the opened cigarette case first to Mrs. Landin and then to Cherry.

"Oh, thank you. I wouldn't know how to smoke a cigarette," Mrs. Landin said, flustered.

"I would," said Cherry, speaking for the first time. "But I won't have one just now, thank you."

Mrs. Landin's eyes nearly fell out of her head. She remembered just in time that Cherry was seeking to be employed by this man who was so nonchalantly offering cigarettes around. She closed her mouth in a line that was half sad, half determined.

"You also swim very well, Miss Landin," Stephen Denton said, resuming his chair. As he lit his cigarette he looked up at her suddenly. "I have seen you down at the beach."

"I have seen you too, Mr. Denton," Cherry said, surprised at her own composure. "I am sorry we have not met before."

He bowed his head in recognition of her small politeness.

"We've wasted rather a lot of time, haven't we?" he said. His eyes, quick and shaft-like, looked across the room at her. Cherry was certain there was a smile in the depths of those eyes. She was sure he was laughing at both of them now. There was nothing that Stephen Denton actually said or did that made Cherry feel that he was amused. Yet intuitively she knew that if it hadn't been for the amusement he found in this ménage he would have been frankly bored.

Well, if he took her up on that station she would show him she really was a modern girl, in spite of the adverse appearances now. Dad had given her ten pounds. And she had fifty pounds in her savings bank account. She would buy slacks and pullovers, and coloured flatties for her feet, like the other girls!

With a sudden extraordinary sense of release Cherry wondered why she had never done that before. Maybe *she* could have educated her parents. Maybe she was the one who should have shown them how life had changed since they were young.

Moreover, Cherry was already wondering why she felt

the ice thaw from her heart when he had said the little girl Sandra was not his child, and that he was not married. Nevertheless he had said he could rectify his state of single blessedness at any moment. That meant he was engaged, or at least had a girl friend.

Girl? Would she be a girl, Cherry wondered. He would be more than thirty, wouldn't he? This girl, this nebulous person he could leg-rope into matrimony just when it pleased him, would probably be older than herself. To nineteen anything older than herself was very hoary indeed – if female.

"You would like to come to Yulinga?" Stephen Denton was asking, his eyes once again swiftly but imperceptibly appraising her. "We have a swimming tank, and a water-hole in the creek. Is that inducement enough?"

There was no smile but something in his eyes told Cherry he was laughing again. Why didn't he ask was she good at teaching? Was she prepared to go so far away? Could she stand up to the harsh climate of the outback?

He was asking none of these things. Instead he was referring obliquely and personally to the fact that he had seen her swimming often, that he had noticed she was a good swimmer. He had not forgotten this was the girl he saw, quite often, down there on the golden sands at the foot of the street. . . .

"I would like to go to Yulinga very much because I would like to have charge of Sandra," Cherry said a trifle primly.

A small muscle moved in Stephen Denton's cheek.

Oh, well! Why did she have to bother what he thought of her at all? She wouldn't have to work for him. It would be his brother and his brother's wife that mattered. And Sandra too.

The tall man who sat sun-baking on the beach had gone for ever, and in his place was this other man, easy, composed, subtly twisting herself and her mother into making themselves look foolish for his entertainment.

He was just as attractive as that other man, it was true,

but Cherry, sitting straight-backed in her chair, would never let him do this to her again. Of that she was certain.

Just wait till she broke loose with that fifty pounds, not to mention the ten-pound note, in that fashion shop along the Highway where all the girls bought their slacks and shuffle shoes, and backless swimsuits.

Cherry looked past Stephen Denton to her mother. Suddenly she knew it was not only her nineteenth birthday, but she *was* grown up. Her parents had opened the cage of youth and invited the bird to go out into the world.

Cherry felt at that moment, far more than she had when she had woken early in the morning, that she truly stood on the doorstep of the gilded cage. Her wings were quivering for their first flight.

She would shed these quiet decorous clothes that were always worn an inch too long, and the shoes that were never quite one thing or the other, but breathed of quality, endurance and a polished life that went on for ever.

She would be a bird with gay plumage.

"Yes, Mr. Denton," she thought, looking at him, unaware of the unexpected challenge in her eyes, the quick joyous uplift of her head. "Just wait till I get loose in that shop. You won't ever laugh at me again."

CHAPTER THREE

Two weeks later Cherry was aloft in the M.M.A. Fokker Friendship plane heading for the north-west. She had a thousand miles to go up the coast, and then by a small feeder plane inland to Yulinga Station.

In her larger case, stored in the freight compartment, were those gaily coloured " stoves." The saleswoman in that fashion shop in the Highway had done some educating of Cherry.

"The trade name is, of course, slacks. But you'll find your friends will call them 'stoves' because of the stovepipe legs."

There was a biscuit-coloured cotton pair, a dark green

pair, for knockabout, and a heavenly pair of damson red velvet for "occasions". Cherry hadn't any idea what those occasions would be but the salesgirl had assured her they would occur and the lovely velvet form-fitting slacks were a " must."

Then had followed the gay array of cotton blouses, some without sleeves and with pretty frills.

A dressmaker had been called in by the willing but bewildered Mrs. Landin and Cherry's beautiful quality silk and cotton dresses had been recut in more fashionable line and length. To crown her dark unruly hair there had been a biscuit-coloured coolie straw hat and a small velvet thingummy for that special "occasion" the salesgirl had promised her. For her feet there were thongs, suède casuals and one pair of Italian high-heeled shoes.

Stephen Denton was in a seat in the forward part of the plane and occasionally when Cherry could drag her eyes from the colourful wonder of the earth beneath to look at the back of his head she felt somewhat grateful for the fact he had been quietly laughing at her that day he had come to the house.

It had taken just that to jolt Cherry into true independence. Yes, she hadn't altered her opinion that he was a superior if fascinating man in a godlike kind of a way, but he had done her a service when he had smiled inwardly at her and smiled outwardly at her mother.

She would show him from now on there was nothing to laugh at, or pity, in the Cherry Landin who was heading for Yulinga and who would take charge of young Sandra Denton.

She had boarded the plane in a simple linen frock with the coolie hat on her head at a jaunty angle.

She had been pleased to see the quickly veiled surprise in his eyes as he had risen from the deep arm-chair in the airport lounge as she had come in before the plane left.

Cherry's hat was not the only jaunty thing about her. So was her honey-coloured satchel bag and the vagabond cut the hairdresser who worked next to the fashion shop had given her. It made her look just a little cheeky in a charming way and as Cherry had never been, let alone looked, cheeky before, this complete change gave her an excited kind of confidence.

"And wait till he sees the rest of my hair piled up on the top of my head," she thought. "He'll understand that the Street of the Pines is no longer thirteen thousand miles from Paris. It's only two days by air."

Stephen Denton had preceded Cherry on to the plane and found her seat for her. He put her hand baggage on the rack and brought the hostess, whom he evidently knew well, and committed Cherry to her care.

"I'm going up forward," he said. "I know both pilots and we like to put the affairs of the pastoral world to rights on a long trip like this. Miss Sands will look after you but if there is anything I can do for you, let me know."

It was a wonderful trip, smooth as a butterfly flying through silken air except on the short trip across a bay when they left Carnarvon.

Below, on the starboard side, the red earth flowed away mile upon thousand mile into incredible distances. On the port side was the sea coast, with its curves and bays, its gold, green and blue seas into which there occasionally emptied the iron-grey water of the snakelike rivers.

Cherry had never imagined such colours. Why, she wondered, hadn't someone ever painted them? Or was there a paintbox anywhere that could contain such colours?

When they came down at the ports – three times they landed on station strips apart from major ports – Cherry was able to get a closer glimpse of the land. The earth was the same startling red but the clumps of mulga trees and spinifex, the dryness of that red earth, were a little frightening.

Not once through that long day did Stephen Denton come near Cherry. He had satisfactorily, if safely, wiped his hands of her when he had committed her to the care of the hostess. There had been nothing she needed but she nevertheless thought his aloofness was not exactly chivalrous or kind. Not that she wanted him to come near her, of course. All the same . . .

She laughed to herself. She was not being very logical, she knew, but there it was. He was a strange man, one who both attracted and repelled her. In a more reflective moment, she wondered why this was so.

It was sundown, with a glorious sunset over the red sea and against a flame, purple and aquamarine sky, when they landed at Dampier and changed to a small Dove plane for the trip inland. Again Stephen Denton was forward and Cherry aft. There was no hostess on this small plane but Cherry was tired now and when the colour had gone out of the world she fell asleep in her seat. If he looked to see if she needed anything she didn't know.

Cherry had been fourteen hours in the air and had become so used to the landing and taking off, in spite of the thrumming in her ears each time they came down, that when the plane landed on Yulinga she remained dozing in her seat unaware of journey's end.

Stephen Denton had to rouse her by gently shaking her shoulder. The air flight had begun to take its toll on Cherry now and she looked up at him dazedly. Where was she? And, heavens, what did she look like?

The coolie hat had long ago been shelved on the rack. The plane was not pressurised so the heat had brought discomfort not only to Cherry but to her clothes. Her linen dress must be crushed beyond all hope of achieving a smart, let alone a dignified, effect, she feared. Her hair felt damp on her scalp and she knew it was sticking in unhappy strands to her temples.

Stephen, coatless and with the stock gone from his open-necked shirt, looked cool and master of himself. Cherry could have cried for what she thought must be a sad comparison. Besides, she was hollow in the stomach. This must be some mild form of air-sickness for she had had plenty of refreshment throughout the day.

"I guess I look green," she thought. "And of course I *am* green, going to sleep like that without giving myself a chance to tidy up before we land."

She followed Stephen to the gangway and down the miniature flight of steps to the ground, where she stood blinking in the glare of truck and car lights. There were three vehicles, she thought. Vaguely she wondered why it took three big motor cars to collect Stephen and herself, for they were the last passengers to leave the plane.

Stephen and the air-pilot had carried her hand luggage and case out of the plane and they now put it with Stephen's bags on the ground. There were a number of men about and when Cherry had gathered her wits she counted seven of them. They were grouped in the small space of the car lights and Cherry could feel that the shadows beyond those headlights stretched out and around them for ever, never reaching anything and going on, in all directions, to infinity.

That had been her last thought about the pindan, streaked with red earth tracks, as the Dove had circled Dampier and then flown out eastwards into the heart of the continent.

A tall, slim man, dressed in tight-fitting drill trousers, and open-necked shirt was speaking.

"How are you, Stephen? Everything all right down below? How's the house? Fit for habitation? See you brought the girl with you."

Cherry couldn't see his face for his back was to the headlights of the parked cars.

Three other men were talking to the pilot and in the still night air, beyond the voice of the man talking to Stephen, she could hear the metallic drawling of their voices.

Stephen turned to her.

"Well, here you are, Miss Landin. Here's your boss. My brother, Hugh Denton."

A long arm came forward and a hard hand gripped Cherry's hand.

"Glad you've come, Miss Landin. Guess you're tired after that trip. We'll pack you up in the overlander straight away." He turned and called to the other group, "Algy, get the Thermos out of the wagon, will you? Guess we'll have some tea before we start. Ben, pack Miss Landin away in my bus, will you. Stow her luggage in the back. She can have a nap while we're passing the Thermos."

Did she look as sleepy and dazzled by the lights as all that? Cherry wondered. Nevertheless, she was glad to follow the man called Ben to the long streamlined station wagon drawn up at the side of the strip. He was another tall lean man but he was wordless. He opened the front door and held it while Cherry got in and after shutting it began immediately to move her luggage from the pile under the plane's wing into the back of the wagon.

The night was warm and very still. Through the window on the far side Cherry could see into the purple world beyond the dazzle of lights. It looked like a vast black ground-map hooded with a sky so brilliant with stars it was like something painted in a tropical dream.

She turned her eyes back to the circle of light.

The men were now in a circle, sitting back on their heels, while one poured tea from a flask into a group of mugs on the ground. They were talking about mobs and bores and the price of cattle.

The man who poured the tea brought a mug over to Cherry and passed it to her through the window.

" Here you are, miss. Pipin' hot."

" Thank you," Cherry said gratefully. It was black tea with no sugar yet somehow it revived Cherry a little.

" How odd," she thought, " sitting here in a car in the middle of nowhere while those men sit there talking to one another as if I didn't exist."

This was Cherry's first experience of this feminine exclusion from men's talk.

The tea was finished, dregs were emptied on the ground and the mugs and flask put back in " Algy's " car.

The pilot climbed back into the plane and suddenly all its fairy lights died as he extinguished them. He then climbed out again, folded the steps back into the body, and slammed the door shut.

He came towards the station wagon with Stephen and Mr. Hugh Denton. Without ceremony they all got into the car.

28

"I'll drive, Hugh," Stephen said and he got in beside Cherry.

"Had another nap?" he asked, looking at her by the light of the dashboard.

Cherry shook her head.

"No," she said. "I was too interested——"

He had put the key in the ignition switch but he did not turn it. Cherry's words seemed to have surprised him.

"In what?" he said. "You're on Yulinga but you're in the middle of nowhere. There's nothing but anthill and sand to see for miles around."

"There was the plane, with its lights on, sitting there on the ground. It was very pretty. And that sky with all the stars. And you men drinking tea in a circle, all sitting on your heels——"

"What's odd about that?"

Cherry was silent a minute.

"Well, you'd never know," she said. "You're too used to it. It's something I've never seen before."

He turned the key and started up the engine thoughtfully. Hugh Denton and the pilot were talking to one another in the back seat. Their voices were quiet, a murmur against the engine.

"Well, well," said Stephen. "So you found that interesting!"

Cherry could not tell him that as she had watched that scene from the car window she thought of the father she had never known. How often had he done that in the long ago before she was born? Had he sat on his heels like that? Emptied the dregs of his cup on an airstrip? Had he been tall and brown-skinned with hard hands and a soft drawling voice like these men? Looking at them had she been looking at the prototype of her own father?

"Well, what do you think about it now?" said Stephen later as he stepped up the pace and the car swung through a dust haze along a red track between the dark shadows that must have been spinifex.

"I wasn't thinking of it. I was thinking about a man," said Cherry, still a little saddened by the thought of that

29

father who was, paradoxically, both nebulous and real in this empty half-lit world.

Stephen held the wheel with one hand while he fumbled for a cigarette, found it and lit it. He drew on the cigarette then glanced sideways and downwards at Cherry.

"Homesick?" he asked. Was that mockery or kindness in his voice? Cherry preferred to think it was the former.

"I'm very happy to be here," she said firmly. "In about twelve months' time I'll start to get homesick."

"You might like the north. Some do, you know. It gets them like a disease. They can't leave it." He was being objectively pleasant.

"Not me," said Cherry. "You see, I've promised and that promise means more to me than anything else on earth."

"Hmm. Sounds like a man, again."

"It is," said Cherry. "The nicest man in the world." Then she added a trifle defiantly, for she felt sure that Mr. Stephen Denton's attitude to her parents was still one of faint incredulity, "I love him. And in one year's time I shall go back to him. I've promised but even if I hadn't promised, that is what I would want to do."

Stephen swung the wagon round a curve, still with only one hand on the wheel. With the other hand he flicked away the ash of his cigarette into the tray in the dashboard. Cherry had looked at him as she had spoken and she could see the sudden raised eyebrows and the quick amused bow of his mouth. He lifted the cigarette and drew on it again, taking a long time to expel the shaft of smoke.

"Must be quite a man," he said, a mixture of astonishment and amusement in his voice.

"He is," said Cherry emphatically.

Then she put a rein on herself.

What could it possibly matter to him what she thought about Dad? Why was she trying to impress him, for that was what she really was doing. In some oblique way she was defending her parents against no spoken accusation.

Let him think what he wanted. Besides, he was the

brother of her employer, she couldn't afford to antagonise him. He probably wouldn't care anyway. He was only talking to her now for politeness' sake though heaven knows, that kind of politeness had been absent from their relations since they had left Perth airport at six o'clock in the morning.

"What am I worrying about?" thought Cherry, irritated with herself. "Maybe this is a very big station. Maybe I won't even see him again, except in the distance."

CHAPTER FOUR

It was indeed a very big station as Cherry was already beginning to discover. They had half an hour's fast driving through that dark magical night before they came to the homestead. Again the motion of the car and the silence that had now descended between them made Cherry feel sleepy. She was also drugged with changing altitudes, changing climates and long flying hours.

If she kept her eyes open all she could see was the shafts of light from the headlamps lighting up a red track and moving in a flickering dance of yellow motes against the background of dark nothing that stretched on either side of them. There were no trees, otherwise the lights would have picked them up. There was nothing but the great bowl of night, the red track and themselves moving through the desert land.

She closed her eyes. That way she could shut herself away from thought of the man next to her. He had made his small sporadic gesture at conversation, done his duty, and was now preoccupied with the business of driving the car to the station homestead at great speed. Once, when she glanced sideways, she noticed he was frowning.

The swinging motion of the car told Cherry they had turned a corner. A minute later the car braked and came to a standstill.

There was the sound of dogs barking on the night air, and a minute later two kelpies were at the doors.

"Quiet, Blue! Quiet, Darkie!" Hugh Denton said from the back seat as he swung open the side door and put his long legs out of the car on to the ground. He straightened up.

The dogs were instantly quiet, they stood rigid, their eyes watching the dark shadow of their boss. Not even their tails wagged.

Cherry amidst a blur of first impressions was very surprised at the dogs. Hugh Denton had spoken so softly, and the dogs had obeyed instantly.

Stephen wasted no time after he brought the car to a stop. He pulled on the handbrake with one hand and opened the drive door with the other. He got out and walked round the bonnet of the car as if to open the passenger's door for Cherry but already his brother had done this. Stephen, a tall dark shadow, stopped in the lights of the car, took out a cigarette and after lighting it threw the match down on the ground with a flick of the wrist. He turned to the air-pilot who meanwhile had got himself out of the wagon by the far door.

"You don't smoke?" Stephen said more as a statement than a question.

"No," the young pilot laughed. "Don't smoke, drink or swear. But I've one vice. I like the ladies."

He joined Hugh Denton in removing Cherry's baggage from the very rear seat of the car.

Cherry could see they had come to a stop at the homestead steps. Right beside them those three steps led up to a wide veranda. The front door and all the windows of the house stood wide open and uncovered so that, standing there beside the car, Cherry had a feeling she was seeing everything that belonged in that lighted house.

The front door opened straight into a large living-room decorated lavishly with indoor pot-plants and ferns. A small fair-haired woman was quietly crossing the floor, coming towards the door. The new governess was not sending this woman whoever she was, into a flurry of excitement; that was for certain.

In a front room at the side of the house a slim girl had just risen from a chair in front of a Transceiver set. She stretched, her hands reaching up towards the ceiling in an abandoned ballet-like gesture. She had red hair falling in smooth waves to her shoulders. Cherry could not see her face but could see the other girl wore a white silk overblouse and shining midnight-blue slacks.

The sight now of the girl in that gorgeous pair of slacks caused Cherry to expel her breath with relief. She had been right. Slacks were the right thing to wear even here.

It was nice, too, to feel there was someone her own age about. Stephen Denton had not mentioned this. But then, he hadn't mentioned very much at all. Summed up, all he had said amounted to a swimming tank, a creek, his brother and sister-in-law, a little girl and a baby.

Cherry, standing quite still beside the car, was fascinated by that glimpse into the heart of someone else's house. She realised the three men were still talking about cattle and droughts and this station and that station as they took the baggage and put it in a pile below the veranda steps.

"Well, you have arrived!" It was the pilot smiling at her through the filtered light that shed a path out into the night from the house.

"Yes, so I have," said Cherry, coming to herself. She smiled back. "What happened to the other men? The ones drinking tea with you at the plane."

"They're from the Yulinga outcamps. They don't live up this way. 'Bout twenty-five miles t'other way. They came in for the mail."

The two brothers Stephen and Hugh were standing talking to one another as if Cherry did not exist and as if getting home and into the homestead was nothing compared with the state of the station first and the nation last. They talked to one another in voices that were quiet and had no emphasis whatever.

They were curious people, these Dentons, Cherry thought.

33

One minute they were so quick in their movements, and quick in their decisions too, and the next they were taking all the time in the world to settle their conversational affairs.

Moreover, very clearly, they had forgotten the new governess was here.

"You stay at Yulinga overnight?" Cherry was asking the pilot politely. She did not quite know what to do next. The Denton brothers had forgotten her, and she could hardly take herself, uninvited, up those three steps and across the veranda.

"That's right. Take off at sun-up to-morrow for Rushing Downs and Darwin."

The fair woman inside the house had arrived at the front door now.

"Oh, do come in," she said. Her voice was pleasant; she raised it a little as she said, "Did you bring Stephen with you, Hugh? And the governess?"

"I've got her right here," the pilot answered instead of Hugh Denton. "Come on, Miss Landin, you must meet Mrs. Denton."

He took her arm in a friendly way and assisted her up the steps. Curiously Cherry felt she did need that friendly gesture and that helping hand. She was suddenly tired to the point of collapse. When she spoke to the pilot she knew her voice was husky with exhaustion.

Mrs. Denton opened the wire screen door and came out on to the veranda. The light was behind her now and Cherry could not see her face clearly but she got the impression of a small, slight woman, slender-boned and perhaps frail.

"I'm so glad you've come," Mrs. Denton said. "I don't feel as if I could carry on much longer without some help for Sandra and Peter. Not that Sandra's any trouble. She's not, but I've got to get Peter into the Flying Doctor base for his injections sometime in the next week or two before we're cut off by the Wet." She looked up at Cherry inquiringly. "You're not very old, are you? I do hope you won't find it too lonely here. It's so hard to keep white girls for long. Did you have a good trip?"

"Yes, thank you, only it was very long——"

"Of course it is. Well, you must sleep in to-morrow." Mrs. Denton looked past Cherry.

"Hugh," she said again, "are you two ever coming in? Tracy's here and bursting for a glimpse of Stephen."

The two men, on the other side of the car, who did things sometimes fast and sometimes slow, now moved into action.

"Righto, Betty," said Hugh, straightening himself up from where he had been leaning against the hood of the car.

Stephen swung about and came round to the foot of the steps.

"Hallo, Betty," he said. He smiled at his sister-in-law as he mounted the steps. "You'll like your new house down south. Big, airy, and a stone's throw from the beach."

He glanced at Cherry.

"Isn't that so, Miss Landin?"

"Yes," said Cherry, eager to convey good news to this woman who seemed to be in need of it. "It's one of the old colonial homes and they are lovely inside. Big high-ceilinged rooms, you know——"

She was suddenly aware of the slim dancer-like figure of the red-haired girl in the blue velvet slacks standing in the doorway. Again the light was behind her and her face, a white oval, was not very clear. Her hair, however, was like fire against the backdrop of that lighted room which had trailing fernery in every nook and corner. And her figure, young, smooth and perfect in its symmetry, was a silhouette any artist would like to capture on paper.

Cherry forgot to go on with her description of that house on the other side of the Street of the Pines from her own home. She was watching Stephen drop his sister-in-law's hand and turn his head to look at the girl in the doorway.

"So Tracy's here," he said softly. Cherry could not see his face but she thought he was probably smiling. "In good health, I see."

"Come inside and see for yourself," the girl said.

With one hand she opened the wire screen door, then turned sideways so that her back leaned against the door jamb. She rested her head against the woodwork so that her chin was lifted. Her profile was exquisite. She raised one knee and slid the sole of her foot upwards until it rested against the woodwork of the door frame. It was an alluring though casual pose.

Stephen said nothing though Cherry was sure that he again smiled.

This, then, was the girl. He had said he could marry her any moment if that was what would qualify him in Mrs. Landin's eyes to take Cherry a thousand miles up the coast and several hundred miles inland.

He had been joking, of course, but there was always a seed of truth in every joke. There are always nuances about the relationships between two other people. This girl, whose name was Tracy, didn't mind one atom that those nuances now announced to the group on the veranda that she was interested in one person only. That person was Stephen Denton. She didn't even glance at the new governess.

Mrs. Denton put her hand on Cherry's arm.

"Well, come inside," she said. " I've some supper ready, then I expect you'd like to go to bed. Time enough in the morning for the children." She turned to lead the way into the house. " If you two would mind remembering there are other people in the world and they'd like to go through the door," she said, addressing Tracy and Stephen, who were talking to one another and obstructing the doorway. " Oh, Miss Landin, I haven't introduced you to my sister, Tracy Evans . . . Tracy, this is Sandra's governess, Miss Landin."

"Cherry Landin," Cherry amended gently, then added, " How do you do?"

The only thing Tracy moved was her head. She turned it to look at the newcomer.

"I suppose you're frightfully tired," she said in an affected voice that implied this statement was the only conversation necessary to offer someone who had travelled so far since early morning. " Aeroplanes bore me to screams," she added.

" Would you mind moving, Tracy," Mrs. Denton asked again. " You've got a whole month in which to talk to Stephen, and roughly half a million acres in which to do it. We would like to go in through the door, please."

Tracy laughed. She let her foot slide down the door jamb until it touched the ground then with a flick of her shoulders she turned into the house. Cherry decided that Tracy's back view in those " stoves," as she moved nonchalantly across the room, was the most seductive thing in the world.

Now, in the full light, and when Tracy turned round and slid backwards and downwards into an easy cane chair, Cherry decided that *seductive* was the emotive adjective descriptive of the whole of Tracy, back and front.

Not the least of the striking things about the girl were her face and hair. The bone structure of her face with its high cheekbones, short straight nose and pointed chin was unusual. It was made up with something white and opalescent so that it glowed. Her eyes and eyebrows were beautifully marked by soft shadow-shading of blue, and yes, green make-up. Her lips were outlined with a pale pink lipstick that somehow did not conflict with the deep glowing red of the hair that looked so casual as it swept down her cheeks, nearly to her shoulders, and yet did not have one shining hair out of place. Also it looked as if it had been dusted with some glow from the last of the sunset.

Cherry was terrifically impressed and just a little awed by the other girl's magnificent, careless sophistication.

She had now slung her legs over the arm of the chair so the midnight-blue velvet slacks added to a vivid and tantalising colour scheme.

Cherry had seen models who looked like Tracy Evans; and magazine covers; and Kim Novak in the films. She'd never dreamed of finding such a person in the middle of a red earth desert on an outback cattle station.

"You look like a witch's brew," said Stephen, coming into the room and smiling down at Tracy. "A very be witching brew, I had better amend hastily."

"So nice of you to like it," said Tracy casually.

"Would you like to sit down," Mrs. Denton asked Cherry pleasantly and ignored her sister, "or would you prefer to see your room and have a wash-up. You look tired . . ."

"And dusty," Cherry added for her. "I would like jus a few minutes to tidy myself, if you don't mind . . ."

"Well, come along. Your room is the end one on the left down this short passage. You'll find the shower-room through the french window at the end of the veranda."

She turned and spoke to her husband who had just come into the living-room.

"Hugh, will you turn the light on in the side veranda for Miss Landin? And you men, please use the tank shower room——"

As she drew aside the hanging cane curtain which covered the doorway into Cherry's room she added :

"Have your shower now and then slip on something light so you can go to bed straight after we've had some supper. You look as if you're nearly dropping."

"I am," thought Cherry to herself, but aloud she said, "Thank you very much."

"The children are asleep so you'll have to wait till morning to see them," Mrs. Denton added. She preceded Cherry into the room and looked round swiftly as if to see if she had forgotten anything in the preparation of the room. She turned round and smiled.

"I do hope you will like it here," she said.

"I'm sure I will," Cherry said gratefully.

"Come into the living-room when you are ready," Mrs. Denton said as she went out, letting the cane curtain fall across the door with a musical rustle.

Cherry, dazed with tiredness, looked round the room.

"In the morning," she said to herself, "I'll really get to know you."

It wasn't the lovely modern cosy grey and pink of her

own room at home. It was old-fashioned and the walls were papered with some dark floral design. It was not a big room but it held a wardrobe, a dressing-table and a book-case full of books. Cherry noticed them with pleasure but looking at their titles was something beyond her now.

The floor was covered with a shining linoleum in dark colours and on either side of the bed, which looked com-fortable, were sheepskin mats. The most interesting feature was the doorways, opposite one another, the far one leading on to the veranda. They were both covered with full-length cane curtains that hung in a myriad of vertical pieces of cane, strung together with beads. As Mrs. Denton had shown her into the room, and again when Mrs. Denton had left, the curtains made a pretty tinkling sound.

The atmosphere was warm so Cherry guessed that the reason for the open windows and doors was to allow the con-stant free passage of air. The cane curtains gave privacy but allowed for coolness. Later she found the only door that was capable of being shut and fastened was the shower room. She discovered this to be along a veranda which was a green tunnel of ferns. These enclosed growing plants stood about on wooden stands and hung from the rafters in wire baskets. It was cool, exotic and exciting.

It was all so different from anything Cherry had ever seen she felt sure she was going to enjoy living in this homestead – once she could open her tired eyes wide enough to appreciate it all.

Putting something light on for supper was a problem. Cherry thought wistfully of her own velvet slacks but some-how wasn't sure whether this was right for " the governess " on her first evening. Tracy Evans belonged to the family so she was in a different position. Cherry finally put on a simple button-through cotton dress, slipped on her scuffs over bare feet, combed her hair quickly and neatly and put on a minimum of lipstick.

As she went to the door she had second thoughts about that make-up.

She was here more than a thousand miles from home and beginning a new life. She wanted to begin a new personality too. She couldn't match Tracy with her make-up because she wouldn't know how to go about it. But she could add something a little daring for the prissy miss who had sat in her parents' living-room on the day of that interview.

Cherry took from her bag the new vanity case she had bought herself. It had been a secret and self-conscious buy, yet it had been something her heart had hankered for.

She let the shining black and silver lid spring back and stood looking rapturously at its contents. Miraculously her tiredness temporarily disappeared. In that little case lay all the enchantment of the world. It was Pandora's box and the imps were colours arranged like a paintbox to be used either for rubbing delicately into the cheeks or around the eyelids. There was a mascara pencil in a gilt case and an eyebrow pencil to match it. There were three of the latest shades of lipstick and in the centre a square block of *crême* powder which one applied sparingly with the fingertips.

Cherry, one night at home after her parents had gone to bed, had tried them all out. She hadn't achieved Tracy's exotic and professional look but she had had results that had made her skip round her room – in her new velvet slacks and new casual hair-cut – with the sheer joy of being free to be modern.

How much dared she put on now without being too amateurish about it.

A slight . . . oh, ever so slight an application of the *crême* powder perhaps! And the eyebrow stick to make her eyebrows fly out just a weeny bit towards her temples. Not too much, but just a promise of what she might do some day when she really let her head go.

She was a new person in a new place, wasn't she? All right, she would look new too!

Cherry spent another ten minutes in front of the mirror and the results pleased her greatly. She had forgotten all about being tired and thought the brightness of her eyes was due to the make-up.

She went out of her room, letting the cane curtain drop

back to its own merry tune and walked down the passage which led directly into the living-room.

They were all sitting about drinking tea. On a small table were some sandwiches charmingly decorated with threads of lettuce and rings of capsicums. It was a light supper but all that anyone would need at this hour.

As Cherry came into the room the three men rose slowly, unfolding long legs, but they went on talking to one another without looking at the newcomer.

Cherry was a little disappointed. She was a new person and she would have liked someone to notice it. Mrs. Denton was busy adding water to the teapot from the hot water jug and Tracy did not look up from the magazine she was flicking through.

"It is quite clear," thought Cherry ruefully, "that no one cares about my being here at all, except as someone to help with the children. As a personality I just don't *count*."

The men subsided back into their chairs like concertinas folding up and their voices went on and on. It was all about station affairs. Cherry, as she sat down, wondered what Mrs. Denton and Tracy thought about this exclusion from men's affairs. They, undoubtedly, were used to it.

Mrs. Denton brought Cherry a cup of tea and put the sugar and plate of sandwiches on a small table beside her.

"There you are," she said. "I do hope that will refresh you."

"Thank you very much," Cherry replied. "You are very kind."

She lowered her eyelids as she lifted her cup to her mouth because at that moment Tracy looked up. Cherry rather anxiously expected a silent criticism from the other girl at her own amateurish make-up.

"I like your hair-do," said Tracy in her slow stage-voice.

Cherry's eyelids flew up. This was praise indeed.

"Thank you," she said warmly. Then she smiled at the other girl. "I like yours too."

"It suits me," said Tracy languidly. "Of course it's *out* now but I rather care for the look of myself this way.

Of course I can get it up in a chignon – and do sometimes." She took a cigarette from a box on a table beside her chair and lit it, then blew smoke long and shadowy towards the ceiling. "Irrespective of the fashions," she said loftily, "I think long hair *down* is more attractive. Specially to men."

She looked across the room at the three men.

"Of course any kind of hair-do would drop dead as far as Hugh is concerned," she said. "But then Betty doesn't bother anyhow. But Stephen . . ." She shrugged a shoulder and laughed. She was not looking at Cherry so did not see the astonishment in Cherry's eyes at this forthcoming and illuminating monologue on Tracy's part. Tracy was not only modern in appearance, she was modern in her frankness. She said what she thought and bother who was listening.

"Stephen, of course, thinks he's immune," she said carelessly. "Actually I shall twist him round my little finger, when I'm ready."

Cherry's eyes above her teacup were round with interest. She looked across the room at Stephen. He was lying back in his easy chair, his legs stretched out straight before him, his eyes watching his brother as the latter talked, still in that quiet, flat but not unattractive voice. As Stephen followed these weighty words, whatever they were, he twice brought his left hand up to his forehead and quietly massaged the fingers backwards and forwards across it as if this action was helping thoughtfulness. Maybe he was just tired, as Cherry was, after that long flight. He didn't look it. He was thoughtful, absorbed and a long way from Tracy and her hair-do, as he was from the other female occupants of the room.

"How curious it is," Cherry thought with a sudden insight into the coincidence of this scene, "that here I am, in the same room with that man, more than a thousand miles away from the beach where I used to look at him with such interest. I didn't know then that I would even meet him."

"Tracy has nothing else to do but think about her appearance," Mrs. Denton was saying lightly. "Wait till she's married and has to run a station homestead, a husband and a brother-in-law who work too hard for hours that are too long. And bring up children into the bargain."

Tracy, having disposed of the subject of hair-styles, and probably of Cherry too, picked up a magazine again and examined the cover girl.

"You shouldn't let the aborigines go walkabout," she said briefly, without looking at her sister.

"That is something you don't know anything about," Mrs. Denton said. "I never can persuade people to believe that the natives go walkabout when they want to, and there's no power on earth can stop them. It's to do with their tribal rites."

"You should educate them out of it," said Tracy, opening the magazine. "You've got a perfectly good governess for the children now. You should let her try out her paces on the natives too."

Mrs. Denton looked at Cherry with an air that was a mixture of impatience, despair and resignation.

"I just wish I could," she said. "Miss Landin——"

"Cherry Landin," Cherry said again for the second time since she had arrived. She said it carefully and gently in case the Dentons would not care to call her by her Christian name. She had to give them the opportunity to do so, if they wished.

"I shall call you Cherry then," Mrs. Denton said. "It's rather a nice name. What was I saying? Oh, I remember. The natives are all walkabout just now. You know what that means? They just pack up, put on their corroboree paints, and go off heaven knows where for some sort of tribal gathering. They don't come back for weeks. So I'm afraid you'll find us in something of a pickle. It's always like this when they're walkabout. Still, if you'd take the children off my hands——"

"I'd love to do that," said Cherry. "That's what I'm here for."

"Good," said Tracy, suddenly throwing the magazine down and standing up. She stretched again as Cherry, through the open window, had seen her stretching before. It was a stretch that was as pretty as a dancer's pose.

"Very good indeed," Tracy added, coming down out of her stretch. "That takes young Peter off my hands at mealtimes. Cherry, he takes his own time to eat five meals a day. That means you can give up half your waking hours to feeding Peter, if you've patience. I'd recommend you stick to Sandra if it didn't mean I'd have to face Peter and that bowl of cereal or that bowl of soup and vegetables myself."

"Wait till you have children of your own," said Mrs. Denton.

They were all three standing now and Cherry was helping gather the used cups and saucers together. When she crossed the space to the men and retrieved their cups they did not stir. Cherry realised this was because they did not notice. They were still talking about the price of beef, sale by weight and grade as against auctioning and the buyer's quote. Women didn't exist for them at the moment. Their entire thinking apparatus was concentrated on thousands of head of cattle and half a million acres of station country.

Cherry decided they were spoilt, and their manners were like their movements, sometimes active and sometimes recuperating.

"I don't intend to lose my figure," said Tracy coldly, in reply to her sister's injunction to wait until she, Tracy, had children.

Whether it was Tracy's words or purely an accident of timing it was impossible for Cherry to say, but at that moment Stephen looked up, then slowly unwound himself and stood up. Hugh, still talking to the pilot, followed suit but didn't know he was doing it. His mind was now in air-freighting beef.

Stephen smiled across the room at Tracy who, having reached the doorway, threw herself into another pose against the door jamb.

"Good night, sweetie," she said to Stephen. "See you in the morning when I can carve you loose from Hugh's edifying conversation. You've got a foam-rubber pillow on your bed. A present from me. I brought it from Sydney." She hooded

44

her lids over her eyes and made a spell-binding gesture with her hand. "Sweet dreams," she added and swung herself gracefully round the door jamb and out of the room.

"Yes, truly," Cherry thought, watching, her own hands full of teacups, "*bewitching,* and Stephen used the right word."

She glanced across at the three men but Stephen had turned slightly away as he went through the process of winding himself up again to sit in that chair. Hugh and the pilot were already down.

They did not look at Cherry nor say "Good night" as she went out.

If she was a piece of furniture, she thought, at least she was a mobile one and would be useful. She came to Mrs. Denton's aid with the washing-up in the kitchen.

A few minutes later, as she went towards her own room, she saw the three men again. They were standing up in the lighted circle of the living-room, obviously preparing to leave it. Hugh Denton was still quietly talking and Stephen stood, both hands in his pockets, gently rocking back on his heels.

He saw Cherry pass by and taking one hand out of his pocket raised it in an easy salute that meant – good night. He actually smiled, and for the first time Cherry admitted he was as attractive as that dream figure she had thought about on those morning swims by the beaches down south.

It warmed her heart, but frightened her a little. She couldn't think why. The picture of him standing there, his hand casually raised, and the brief smile disarming his otherwise preoccupied expression, went with her along the passage to her room.

It stirred her heart, as the sight of forbidden fruit might have done when she was a child.

It was an unexpected, friendly, almost intimate smile yet it came from the heart of a stranger.

45

Several weeks went past with Cherry not only adapting herself to station life but beginning to love it.

Mrs. Denton was a kindly person and Cherry felt a strong bond of sympathy for her. The older woman really did have too much to do when the natives were away and she occasionally suffered from migraine. This meant she was glad to have someone like Cherry to help her with the children.

Sandra was an attractive child, small for her seven years, sunburned, straw-haired and dedicated to an interest in everything that went on about the station to the total exclusion of spelling, arithmetic and anything to do with books.

She was friendly, in a quiet shy way, with Cherry. Often as Cherry worked with her she found the child's attention wandering and her eyes gazing out of the window. Cherry felt a certain pity and understanding for Sandra because her thoughts and dreams were all for the outside world.

Her heart ached when she thought of the child being sent south to boarding school next year. She felt better when she learned that Sandra had been booked into a school that was based on a farm, and that riding was a curriculum subject.

Cherry was conscience-stricken about the little girl because in truth almost all her heart had gone to the baby Peter. This was something not regretted by Mrs. Denton for suddenly her younger round-eyed child with the angelic smile had discovered a fairy godmother. And Cherry had discovered her heart's desire.

Cherry didn't mind sitting three-quarters of an hour in the chair beside Peter's high chair on the veranda, plying him with food in a spoon, while Peter took his time to masticate and swallow, occasionally blowing bubbles at Cherry, rat-a-tatting with his own spoon on the side of his table tray. All the time he favoured Cherry with the most guileless and seraphic of smiles. His large blue eyes beamed on her.

Sometimes he had little chance of getting on with his eating at all because his small, red baby's mouth was parted in delighted laughter.

If ever a child smiled his way into someone's heart, that child was Peter, and Cherry was that someone.

"Oh!" Cherry exclaimed to Mrs. Denton once when she felt that she and Peter were taking just too long in the process of eating and beguiling one another. "I do feel that perhaps I spoil Peter for you. And I should spend more time with Sandra."

This was an occasion when the feeding was going on in the kitchen in the early morning. Mrs. Denton was tidying up, after the men's early morning breakfast.

"Nobody can spoil a baby with companionship," Mrs. Denton said without turning round. "That's what he needs and it's just what I haven't got time to give him. You go right ahead, Cherry. Anyhow Sandra's gone out with her father to the outcamp. He wanted to take her and she wanted to go."

"But you did bring me here for Sandra," faltered Cherry as she wiped Peter's hands and mouth and lifted him out of his chair. Holding the baby in her arms she looked anxiously at Mrs. Denton's preoccupied back. That back was a little stooped this morning and it looked as if another migraine might be impending. If so it was just as well Sandra had gone to the outcamp with her father.

"Enter migraine, exit arithmetic," thought Cherry with sympathy for both Sandra and her mother.

"It doesn't matter what you came here for," said Mrs. Denton in a quiet voice. "The point is, you've taken Peter off my hands. He does love you. I can see that. We can settle down to worrying about Sandra when the natives come back from their walkabout. The lubras will at least do this kitchen and the general housework."

"Shall I take Peter outside now?" asked Cherry.

"Yes, please. Take him out and put him on the floor of the veranda and give him the pegs. He'll stay quietly playing with them for hours. That is, if *you're* not too far away." She turned round. "Perhaps you would do some of the mending for me?" She looked at Cherry anxiously. Mending wasn't governessing, she knew. "I never can catch up with the buttons and frayed collars. Not to mention the holes Hugh and Stephen get in their working pants. It's the loose wire out at the boundaries that does it. They're always jagging their pants."

"Of course I will," said Cherry. "That way I can sit near Peter too." She smiled at Mrs. Denton. "And you know I don't mind an excuse for doing that."

"You're a kind girl," Mrs. Denton said with a grateful smile. "How lucky I am that Stephen chose you."

"Stephen didn't choose me," Cherry thought. "He just came across the road and took the first person available."

Cherry carried Peter out on to the veranda where she put him on his own piece of linoleum square on the floor. She brought him his box of gaily coloured plastic toys and the ordinary laundry pegs. True to form, he took only the pegs. Sometimes it took Peter nearly an hour to get two pegs to fit into one another. Then he would look up, deliver himself of that seraphic smile, heave a long sigh of satisfaction and pull the pegs apart again.

Truly, he was the most heart-winning child.

Cherry collected all the sewing she could find and settled herself at a table nearby, hoping that Peter wouldn't absorb so much of her attention she wouldn't reduce the pile by an appreciable amount.

The day was very hot, but its dry withering heat did not touch Cherry's skin as she sat with Peter. They were enshrined on the veranda which was little more than an arbour of green trailing ferns and pot-plants all dampened by the early morning watering.

She had become used to the great empty distance of the outside paddocks with their red-brown floors and their pale shimmering skies. At the side and back of the homestead were the stockmen's quarters, the store, the meathouse, the smithy and the workshops. They were clustered round the homestead but some distance away. It was a small and busy settlement and over it all, framed in a clump of tall trees planted there at least a generation ago, towered the wind-mill. This drew the water for the household from the underground reservoir. Most prosaically it was called the Number One Bore.

Under the giant frame of the windmill was the swimming tank from which Tracy could now be seen emerging.

Cherry looked up with interest for she had not seen Tracy about the homestead this morning and thought she had gone out with Stephen as she sometimes did when he was going to one of the nearer bores.

At this time of the year, Cherry had quickly learned, the cattle were always feeding round one or other of the bores.

Cherry thought of this a little wistfully as she looked up from her sewing and watched Tracy coming through the garden. She would have loved to go out on to the run to see what it was like, but no one had suggested it. Besides, Mrs. Denton needed help in the homestead.

Tracy stepped up on to the veranda, dropped a wet swim-suit on to the floor and with an air of subtle laziness lowered herself into a cane chair nearby.

Her lovely red hair was damp but still neatly in place. Tracy's grooming, though casual, was always perfect. Her white cotton slacks and tiny scrap of a blouse were spotless. Her feet, bare except for flimsy strapped sandals, had the nails of her toes as perfectly painted and polished as if they'd been on her fingers instead.

Though she sat near Cherry she did not look at her; instead she let her large deep-sea eyes gaze out beyond the homestead garden to the vast space of fenceless paddock beyond.

"That house Stephen bought," she said lazily and with-out any preliminary greeting. "What's it like? As good as the awful price he paid for it? I mean——" She shrugged one shoulder and made a small but eloquent gesture in the air with her hand. "Is it *luxurious*?"

"I don't know what it's like inside," said Cherry. She was pleased that perhaps she and Tracy might have some conversation. She had been disappointed in Tracy's indifference to her so far. "But it is a fine old house out-side. By old I mean it was built a long time ago but built very well. You know they did, in those days. And the grounds are lovely——"

Tracy turned her head and looked at Cherry casually.

"How do you know so much about it?"

"I live opposite," Cherry said quietly.

"Oh yes. Of course. I'd forgotten."

There was a long silence which Cherry did not care to break. Tracy rarely had any conversation with her and she felt now that Tracy's coming to sit by her, and asking these questions, meant there was a purpose behind them. She was a little nervous for fear she might say the wrong thing.

"Of course if it's really luxurious," said Tracy airily, "I might consider it."

Cherry hid her surprise by biting off a thread from her sewing. She looked up at Peter who was quite indifferent to Tracy's proximity and who, with a small frown on his brow, was still cogitating the problem of fitting two pegs to-gether. Cherry could not help an involuntary smile. The fate of Peter's whole immediate world hung in the balance. Would the pegs fit, or wouldn't they?

"That is to say," said Tracy, a little piqued that Cherry had not asked her what she meant, "I just might settle down and get married. A house like that makes all the difference between yea and nay, don't you think?"

Cherry was so surprised at this candour from someone who had previously rarely noticed her that she could not hide it.

"But you wouldn't be marrying a house," she said. "You'd be marrying a person, wouldn't you?"

"When you've led the life I've had," said Tracy in a world-weary voice, "you'll understand that a house and a fortune matter very much when you consider giving up a career, not to mention single-blessedness."

For some silly reason Tracy's words gave Cherry a pang. She knew she ought to laugh but somehow the laugh wouldn't come.

"How nice to be some people," she thought.

Cherry had only been one day at Yulinga when she had discovered that Tracy had a flair for ballet dancing. She did her exercises, spinning, curtseying, arabesquing, posing, to the charmed delight of everyone who had time to cast an admiring glance in her direction.

Cherry was able to admire Tracy's beautiful feet, her lovely pointed elbows, the charm and grace of her posturing without jealousy yet with a touch of envy.

How lovely, she thought, to be like Tracy who had, for Cherry, the glamour of the ballerina and stage star.

Yet how curious that Tracy was here, thousands of miles from those lighted stages where surely she belonged.

It must be Stephen.

Whenever Stephen came into the homestead, Tracy was extra bewitching. In a subtle kind of a way Stephen reacted to this bewitching. Cherry could see the odd half-smile, the faint flicker of his eyebrows as he looked at Tracy when he came into the living-room after a bath and change.

Cherry brought her thoughts back to Tracy's words which hung in the air for a moment and Cherry felt she was expected to say something.

"You did ballet dancing in London, didn't you?" she asked pleasantly.

"That's the way I spent my patrimony," said Tracy and again made a sad fateful gesture in the air with her pretty slender hand. She paused. "After that, I was flat broke, except for some fund for which Hugh is trustee. He won't disgorge."

Cherry could not help a gurgle of laughter at the sudden change in Tracy's expression as she said these last words with the air of a tragedy queen.

Peter thought Cherry was laughing at him and he looked up and favoured her with the kind of smile that said:

"Yes, it is fun, isn't it? But I'll get these jolly pegs together sometime before nightfall." He sighed deeply and went industriously back to work.

"Hugh and Betty," said Tracy with a small frown,

51

" consider I ought to settle down and forget London. They, of course, have pots of money but nothing will prise it loose from Hugh."

Cherry was so surprised at this entire conversation she couldn't help wondering why Tracy was confiding her most private affairs to her – when up to date she had shown no interest in the " governess" whatever. She went on sewing and tried to say the right things the right way so as not to offend Tracy on the one hand, nor show too vulgar a curiosity about the financial affairs of the Dentons, on the other.

" He has bought that very beautiful home down there by the ocean——" she ventured carefully.

Tracy threw one leg over the other impatiently.

" Oh, that was Stephen," she said almost irritably. " Of course they're equal partners and Stephen can do what he likes. Perhaps *he* thought the house might be an inducement to me to stay."

" Yes, perhaps he did," said Cherry. " Why don't you ask him?"

" Oh no, no! Not yet," said Tracy. " I haven't quite made up my mind."

She jumped up, went to the balustrade and grasping it with two hands began to do her foot exercises.

She was very pretty, Cherry thought. She had a sprite-like figure and her dancing exercises were graceful and clever.

" Do ballet dancers ever fall in love with *people*?" Cherry asked.

" Oh yes," said Tracy. She lifted one hand from the balustrade and made an airy gesture with it. " Take Stephen, for instance. He's really got something, you know. He really *sends* me. If one could be certain of getting away from the station sometimes – well – that would make the whole difference, wouldn't it?"

" If you didn't like the station life——" began Cherry tentatively.

" My dear, I was brought up on a station," said Tracy.

"The family's lost it now, but what's the odds if I've got this one?"

It seemed that Tracy wanted the best of all worlds, Cherry thought. Her dancing, her station and now her town house that had to be luxurious.

Nice to be some people!

"If I loved a person I'd just go after him and get him, with or without station or town house," said Cherry firmly.

Tracy stopped her exercises and turned round. She looked at Cherry closely.

"Would you?" she said. "Now, would you?" She paused, threw back her hair, dug her hands in the pockets of her slacks and took a step as if to go away. She looked down at the small boy seriously contemplating his unco-operative pegs. She glanced back at Cherry again.

"Peter's the only man round here available," she said. "Too bad he's about twenty years too young."

She picked up her swimsuit and sauntered away. Cherry watching her going.

How odd she, Cherry, should have said anything as silly as that but odder that Tracy had said as much as she had of her own private life. Cherry wondered if there had been an object and if so what was it?

As for herself going after anyone and getting him! She wasn't made that way, alas!

Like Peter contemplating his pegs, Cherry put her head on one side and gazed at her sewing.

"Of course that is what a girl ought to do," she thought. "*Win* her man. One thinks of that way of doing things, but one never does them. Well, for one thing, the man is generally looking the other way. Or it's the wrong man – or something."

She looked up at the scene that lay outside the veranda. Beyond the fence, lit up with the bushes of blazing bougainvillæa, was a trail of horsemen riding out through dust clouds across the endless brown paddocks towards the western sky-line. She wondered where they were going. Where Hugh and Stephen had gone this morning?

One of the things Cherry had liked about station life was that early morning scramble of getting the men off.

Before daybreak there was a thundering of boots about the homestead veranda. Hugh and Stephen appeared in the kitchen, geared like the stockmen for a day out on the run. They wore tan-coloured shirts and heavy drill trousers. Round their waists were wide leather belts that always had a few cartridge heads showing above the seaming. Always one or other of them took a gun. They might see a snake to kill or a 'roo for its hide. Occasionally a bush turkey was brought in as an extra delicacy for the table. Sometimes a bullock, injured by the terrible horns of another beast, had to be shot out of mercy.

Hugh Denton wore spurs as did the other stockmen waiting below the veranda for the morning's instruction, but Cherry noticed that Stephen never did this. She wondered why but didn't like to ask for Stephen took very little notice of her.

Nobody took any notice of anybody at that hour of the morning. Everyone was busy getting the men breakfast . . . and it was an enormous one . . . and getting them away before the sun had been ten minutes above the horizon.

Everyone, that is, except Tracy. Tracy only appeared on those mornings when she was going out with Stephen. These were generally days when he was delayed in the homestead by business in the office. Cherry had been quick to see that Stephen was the business manager. He dealt with the information coming over the Transceiver. He sent and received telegrams. He attended to the mail which came in with the bi-weekly plane.

On those days it was almost mid-morning before he left the homestead and then he occasionally took the truck and went to inspect the nearer bores. Tracy would pack a Thermos and take lunch and go with him.

By this time Cherry was on the veranda with Peter, if Sandra had gone off with her father. She would watch the truck disappearing over the trackless paddock in its own cloud of dust.

Whither were they going? she would wonder. And what

was it like out there beyond the last rise of the paddock? Were there trees and water and places to picnic?

And what did they talk about when together like that?

Cherry had mental visions of Stephen with that slow, assured half-smile of his, the dark grey eyes looking keen, perhaps amused, certainly intelligent, as Tracy talked.

Tracy was a lucky person, Cherry thought. All this and heaven too, because now she wanted a town house and a fortune to add to her talent, her exotic appearance and the apparent conquest of Stephen Denton.

This particular morning Stephen had not gone out with the other men and Cherry had quite expected that he and Tracy had gone somewhere together later.

A period was soon put to her wondering for round the side of the homestead she saw both Hugh and Stephen Denton riding up to the fence. Stephen threw one leg over his horse and slid to the ground, then Hugh followed suit. They came up through the garden together.

Cherry wondered if something was wrong that both brothers should come in before lunch like this.

They came up the steps and along the veranda and stood and looked down at Peter, then at Cherry.

Peter's father smiled in his distant but pleasant way. Stephen, oddly enough, smiled when he looked at Cherry.

" The perfect nursemaid," he said. " Don't you get tired of him, Cherry?"

She shook her head.

" No," she said simply.

The men spoke to her so rarely that she felt embarrassed at the event now. She knew, by this time, that it was shyness on the part of the older brother that kept him so silent : and preoccupation on the part of Stephen. All the same it made her a little nervous about what to say when they did speak.

Hugh coughed, searched in the pocket of his shirt for a cigarette and, still standing there near the child, began to roll a cigarette for himself. He then handed his brother the makings and Stephen did likewise.

The silence was a little unnerving so Cherry bent her

head and went on sewing without exactly seeing what she was sewing.

" Stephen got a call through from Timor Bay this morning," Hugh said slowly, at length. " It's about young Peter. There's a session on up there; innoculating the kids with Salk vaccine. You know about Salk vaccine?"

He looked through a cloud of smoke at Cherry.

She nodded.

" It's an immunisation against polio. All the children down south have had it."

Stephen by this time was sitting down on his heels beside the small boy on the veranda. He held his cigarette with one hand and with the other hand made a third to Peter's two hands. Miraculously the pegs fitted into one another and the long job was done.

Peter sighed deeply, looked at the pegs, then looked up at his uncle. He smiled.

Cherry actually felt jealous.

It was all right for them to smile like that at one another. They were related. She was just the nursemaid. Stephen had said so. She had been meant to be the governess to Sandra, but somehow Peter had changed all that.

Hugh, standing, was still considering his next words. His manner was almost diffident. It was Stephen, sitting there on his heels beside Peter, who took over.

" How'd you like to take this young fellow up to Timor Bay for his injections?" he asked, looking up at Cherry. He smiled encouragingly. " I'm going up on the Northern Airline in a couple of days. Betty doesn't feel up to it and I've a feeling Peter and I'll need you."

Cherry was so startled her heart leapt. Not that she particularly wanted to take another aeroplane ride, let alone go to Timor Bay. But there was something exciting in the fact that the brothers felt she would be capable of looking after the child on such an occasion. And somehow the way Stephen looked up at her seemed to embrace the whole of her with those dark grey eyes and included her in that " Peter and I will need you."

How wonderful to be needed.

Her eyes lit up and the colour deepened in her cheeks.

"Of course . . . of course . . ." she stammered.

She had nearly said, "I'd love to go," and only just stopped herself in time. That would not have been the right way of contemplating a trip that meant poor little Peter would have big needles shot in his arm and that his own mother didn't feel well enough to take him.

On the other hand, there was cause for gladness. They trusted her. All of them. They must have talked it over and Stephen had gone out on the run to bring his brother back to announce the decision to Cherry. After all, Hugh was the father of the child.

That old amused ironic smile came back into Stephen's face.

"Your parents would approve," he said. "Tracy is coming along too. We won't be alone in foreign places."

Now he had spoiled it. Not because Tracy was coming too, of course. But because he had once again laughed at the old-fashioned way she had been brought up.

Cherry pressed her lips together a trifle primly.

"I wasn't thinking of that," she said calmly. "I was thinking that I would like to go very much and that I'll take as much care of Peter as if he were my own. I was also feeling so sorry that Mrs. Denton is not well. It's that migraine again . . ."

"Yes, that's a bad thing," Hugh Denton said slowly. "I'll be taking her down south to that house in February. The change will do her good."

Cherry nodded.

"It's lovely down there by the ocean," she said brightly. "There's always a cool breeze in the evening."

Stephen had risen to his full height again. He was still looking at Cherry but she was trying to look at his brother, not him.

"Beautiful beaches all spattered with beautiful girls," Stephen said and then really laughed at the quick cold look that Cherry gave him.

He turned to his brother.

"Come on," he said. "We'll talk the thing over with

Betty. She'll be relieved that Cherry's going. She knows Tracy is very good at lots of things but not with small boys."

"Er . . . thank you very much . . ." Hugh Denton said a trifle awkwardly to Cherry.

She smiled back at him. He was very shy, this tall out-back cattleman. Her heart quite went out to him. It wasn't an easy thing surely to be trusting his only son to someone who was a near stranger.

It was too bad of Tracy not to feel some responsibility in such a case. After all, Peter was her nephew too.

This thought brought to her mind the picture of two brothers being married to two sisters. Well, quite a good idea when you come to think of it. It was what was called in her psychology text book "the familiar grouping" and was regarded as the very best. People living happily together in families.

All the same, clearly a nursemaid was needed in the Denton family.

When Cherry later spoke to Mrs. Denton about the projected trip she found the older woman greatly relieved.

"I didn't like to ask you, Cherry. A baby that old is a full-time job, but I felt I just couldn't make it. And I'd never forgive myself if anything happened to Peter if he didn't get his vaccine. It's months before the Salk people will be in Timor Bay again."

She hesitated. Her tired grey eyes were already beginning to show, deep in them, the first hard light that meant a bad headache was coming on.

"It's this migraine," she said. "I'll be much better when I've had that break down south. I do love Stephen for having gone to that trouble to go down there and find the house. And fix it up. It was a real sacrifice because he hated leaving the run. So does Hugh, of course. Stephen's much more a man of action when he really gets stirred."

She hesitated.

"It is a nice house, isn't it, Cherry?"

"Lovely," said Cherry warmly. "We live quite near

58

and it's the most beautiful street ever. A double road, you know, with pines down either side and more down the middle between the two roads. They sing in the wind. And they're cool and shady in the hot summer."

Mrs. Denton looked at Cherry curiously.

"I believe you are just a little homesick."

"There is a call from those pines," Cherry laughed. "And the ocean too. Not to mention my parents. But I love the north already, Mrs. Denton. And I think the station life is thrilling. I hope I can go out on the run some day."

"Yes, of course. I'll get Hugh or Stephen to take you when you come back from Timor Bay. You'll only be gone four days, you know."

She had never asked Cherry anything personal about her life before but this sudden decision to put Peter into Cherry's willing charge had unexpectedly brought them a little closer.

"You might make up your mind to stay in the north for good," Mrs. Denton said. She was putting away the silver after the lunch wash-up. She did not look up as she spoke. "That is unless you have some special reason why you would want to go south again. I mean in addition to the call of the pines."

"Well, I did make a promise," Cherry said reluctantly. She too was helping put the things away. She had just reached up to put the plates on the top shelf of the old-fashioned dresser that took up a large portion of one wall of the kitchen. She turned round and looked at Peter, still sitting in his high chair, chewing at a rusk which he held in one hand, and beating a tattoo with his silver spoon on the tray with his other hand.

"It's going to be a tussle between two men," she said, looking at Peter. "That young man there and the north on one hand, and another ever so much older and the pines on the other hand."

"I expect you will have to wait the whole twelve months to see who wins," said Mrs. Denton reluctantly. "Already I begin to wish you would stay on with us, Cherry. But you mustn't sacrifice your own chances in life for other people's lives, you know. Every girl wants to get married some time." She hesitated as she pushed in the drawer of the dresser after the last of the silver had gone in.

"I'm always telling Tracy that. It's time she stopped racketing around the world. She has a wonderful home and security here with Hugh and me. All she's got to do is marry Stephen . . . she'd like marriage then. He's a wonderful person."

Cherry picked Peter up from his chair and wiped his mouth with a small piece of towelling.

"I think I'll put this young man to bed now," she said. "His eyes have got the kind of look that says it's time for an afternoon sleep."

"How quickly you have learned about babies, Cherry," Mrs. Denton said. "I wish Tracy——"

"I wish I had some of the things Tracy has," said Cherry going towards the door. "A lovely figure, beautiful hair. If she loves Stephen she'll marry him in the end. On the other hand, if she is a true artist perhaps it would be kinder to give her an opportunity to use her art."

"She ought to settle down and get married," Mrs. Denton said a trifle stubbornly. "She'd like it if she'd only try it."

"I've got a feeling she will," said Cherry wisely. "She's in love with Stephen, and that's a good start."

"I rather thought so . . ." said Mrs. Denton.

CHAPTER SIX

The pilot who came in with the plane on Sunday night was a stranger because he was flying for a different airline from the one that had flown Cherry and Stephen out of Dampier. His name was Alan Donnelly and the plane was a small twin-engined monoplane.

Cherry was so busy on Sunday, packing for both Peter and herself and at the same time leaving Sandra's clothes in order, that she had hardly time to look at the pilot.

He was above medium height and very nice-looking in his tropical airline uniform.

Tracy was delighted to have some extra male company. Cherry had a vague idea that Tracy was paying overmuch attention to the pilot in the hopes, perhaps, of arousing Stephen's natural possessive feelings. Cherry knew, mostly from her reading and from other girls' College gossip, that some girls made quite an art of this business of pretending an interest in one man in order to impress another.

"Foolish," thought Cherry. "Tracy is so devastatingly attractive, and original, she doesn't have to work hard to impress anyone, anyway. Not Stephen, specially.

"If it was me, now——"

Even her new hair-cut, which by this time was badly in need of a trim, her casual modern clothes and the experiments with the cosmetic case, hadn't quite dispelled from Cherry the conviction that she would never stand out and be noticed in any room.

"Perhaps the prissy miss was my gimmick and I should have stuck to it," she thought ruefully. "A witchery ballerina is certainly Tracy's and she doesn't have to do a single thing about being looked at. One just can't help looking at her."

Thinking of the much-needed hair trim Cherry was glad there would be several days' stop-over in Timor Bay. She hoped there was a good modern hairdresser in that very good modern hotel she had been told about.

Timor Bay was an airport for trans-continental aircraft and catered in the most magnificent tropical way for the great international V.I.P.s flying in and out of Australia. Cherry was hourly becoming more and more thrilled by the prospects of her trip.

Early on Monday morning, the station waggon transported the travelling party, together with the pilot, down the long sloping road to the airstrip which had to be miles away from the homestead because of the falling nature of the ground and the broken, stony surface of the paddocks nearer Yulinga.

Tracy was travelling casually, in slacks and a white sleeveless blouse with the prettiest touch of broderie anglaise at the neck. On her feet she wore a neat pair of black suède flatties as soft-soled and delicate as chamois leather. Her long, sleek, burnished red hair hung down to her shoulders, and in spite of the movement of air because of the travelling car there wasn't a hair out of place. Tracy looked almost "carved" in her outline.

Cherry didn't know what she herself looked like except she wore her new green cotton slacks and a white blouse and had taken time and care over that hair which needed a trim. She was too absorbed with Peter, but she hoped she looked her own best, considering the hour of the morning.

Peter was, she decided, the perfect travelling companion. He had burbled with delight when put into his best blue knickers and white sleeveless shirt. He had sparkled when his white linen hat had been put on his head. He knew he was in for an outing and that a day's adventure lay ahead. Nobody, at that moment, dreamed what an adventure and that it would last more than a day.

Stephen, except for his own personality, looked the prototype of all station owners travelling in the tropical north. He wore well-fitting tan-coloured trousers of fine cloth, a lighter tan-coloured tailored shirt with the same kind of black tie that the pilot wore. In fact the pilot, Hugh Denton, who had driven the station wagon down to the airstrip, and Stephen Denton might have been, until you looked into their faces, triplets grown to the mature age of thirtyish. When they reached the plane, which was sitting alone like a large bird with spread wings, on the ground, the pilot unconsciously disassociated himself from the social likeness to the two brothers by producing out of the plane a pilot's cocked hat. Stephen and Hugh wore their wide-brimmed pastoralists' hats.

They all three looked very distinguished in this informal dress, Cherry thought, sparing a minute from Peter's bubble-blowing, crowing delight. She had a feeling of pride in her countrymen of the north.

Again she had that overwhelming thought, like a nostalgic dream out of former times, that this was what her father must have looked like. Immediately afterwards came the reflection that in this grieving memory she was being disloyal to Dad . . . the dear man who had brought her up as his own child.

As Cherry settled herself in her seat in the plane, she touched the top of Peter's head but at the same time she made to herself the promise not to let Peter so win her heart she did not want to go home to Dad at the end of the year.

Already she could see she was in for heart burning. This, she thought, is the fate of all good nannies. You learn to love other people's children then you have to give them up. It was strange too that she should turn out to be a greater success with Peter than with Sandra. This was a success that Mrs. Denton connived at, for she was so relieved to have the burden of Peter's daily routine taken from her that she already had developed a sanguine attitude that the minimum of Cherry's time would have to be enough for Sandra.

" She doesn't know," thought Cherry with a touch of compunction, " that not only is Peter stealing my heart but I'm very much afraid I am stealing his."

While Cherry was thinking this way she was sitting in the plane, Tracy was over the aisle from her, and Stephen was once again up near the cockpit so he could keep the pilot company.

Perhaps, when Cherry had that thought about stealing Peter's heart, her arms gave him an unconscious squeeze for at that moment Peter turned his head and looked up into her face. He smiled, the guileless smile of a child, that said he had a secret and it was a lovely one.

It was a smile so overwhelming in its trust and charm that Cherry felt as if she had suddenly had a vision of heaven.

Her eyes were a little misty.

" *Oh, Peter,*" she said. She cradled his head against her shoulder and rested her cheek on the top of his small white linen hat. She lifted her eyes and they met Stephen's as, lowering his head to emerge from the cockpit, he glanced her way.

He looked at Cherry. Cherry, too embarrassed at being caught in her little act of endearment to Peter, was unable to take her eyes away from Stephen. Then with a terrible effort she blinked to break the spell, and looked down at the top of Peter's head. Stephen took a step forward and one minute later was asking Tracy if she wanted some magazines.

Cherry had had a thought that had come like an unbidden visitation. She expelled it from her heart and mind at once and tried madly to think of something else . . . anything . . . the whirring of the propellers as they were about to take off – the skidding of the tyres as the plane moved down the runway – the red earth with the grey hummocks of spinifex.

The thought had something to do with that old daydreaming she used to have when she saw Stephen, an unknown magical figure, sitting on the ocean beach near the Street of the Pines. She had never then dreamed that one day she would be flying in a plane with him across the north of Australia.

Cherry felt so guilty at this unexpected audacity on her part she could have cried. Instead she closed her eyes as she now rested her chin on Peter's head and tried to guess the distances from the ground as the plane rose, and the miles per hour they were now travelling.

It was futile guessing, for she knew nothing of heights or speeds, but a concentration on numbers could always send her to sleep when examination-worry had tended to keep her awake in her college days.

How dared she think that way of Stephen Denton! Oh dear, how had such a thought ever come to her?

But what had he been thinking as he came through that gangway? His eyes had looked straight into hers as if he had seen something and recognised something. What? " Oh dear – we must be a thousand feet up now. Perhaps two. How fast do we go to get so high in the sky? Let me see. Somewhere I read that this sort of plane is doing a hundred and fifty miles per hour for the first five minutes after the take-off——"

The thrumming of the plane made Peter sleepy for he

leaned his head back against Cherry and she could see his lids drooping over his eyes.

" Me too, Peter," she said under her breath. " If I sleep I can't think and I'll stop hating myself for such stupidity."

Cherry, with Peter on her lap, leaned her head back against the seat rest and thought of counting clouds since it was silly to count sheep in a part of the country where there were no sheep, only cattle. Since the sky had been cloudless when they'd got into the plane she decided to count cattle.

Whatever it was that Cherry counted it was effective for like Peter, cradled in her arms, she dozed off.

She imagined Tracy, in the midst of her magazines, doing the same thing. She heard Stephen's footsteps come down the aisle of the plane and go back again. She supposed it was Stephen for the pilot, surely, would be flying the plane, wouldn't he?

Anyway Cherry was not going to open her eyes to look at Stephen. In fact she would never look at him again.

How many cattle had she counted? Well, none at all, come to think of it.

Nevertheless Cherry was in a light sleep an hour and a half later when the plane ran into a rainstorm. It wasn't much of a rainstorm and there was very little wind and all the plane did was bucket about somewhat. It didn't wake Peter and it only partially stirred Cherry.

Then the curious unpredictable element that inhabits the upper world above the Australian jungle lands had a striking mood. One minute the plane was flying through still clear air, then it entered the vapour area of a small black cloud which was sailing high and alone like a blue-black ball of cotton-wool in the sky. In its heart was a bolt of electricity waiting for release.

In the somnolent silence of the interior of the plane the sound of the lightning striking the main electrical system of the fuselage was a bolt from the gods.

The plane staggered, then wobbled badly.

Cherry sat upright and Peter in her arms sat upright too.

Nobody uttered a sound for a split second. Then Stephen, who was sitting in the front seat, turned his head.

" Fasten your belts," he said rapidly. " At once."

No flashing sign to fasten belts came from the pilot's cabin because the electrical system was out of action, but neither Tracy nor Cherry noticed this. Stephen's command was enough.

Cherry wondered, somewhat wildly, why her hands didn't tremble. It took quite a time to loosen the buckle of her strap so that it would encompass both herself and Peter.

" We're in this together, darling Peter," she said. " If we're for it – well – you'll be with me."

Even in this momentary emergency she could see Peter's eyes wide open, trying to absorb the fact that something outside his experience was going on that was quite astonishing.

It *was* astonishing, thought Cherry, who was very nearly crying for the future Peter might not have.

Stephen had gone into the pilot's cockpit. The plane wobbled, side-slipped, righted itself, but wobbled again.

All the time Cherry knew by the pressure in her ears they were losing height. She held Peter tightly.

" Five thousand feet, three thousand feet, two thousand feet. Of course I don't really know but thinking of numbers does stop one thinking of something else."

She turned her head and looked across the aisle at Tracy. Tracy caught her glance, shrugged her shoulders, then looked bored.

" How funny," Cherry thought. " We really do die in funny ways, we humans. Tracy bored, and me – well, I could cry for the life Peter might not have. And those two men up there in the cockpit——"

Cherry could not even guess what they were doing or saying.

A map of dark blue-grey caught the edge of her vision and she looked out the window.

Heavens, the earth thick with trees was flying past like a carpet stretched a few feet below them.

"I didn't know there were trees up here," thought Cherry. "It's like a forest, or a jungle or something."

They went over a river and over trees again. The plane wobbled badly as it nosed a little upwards into the wind. The engines were off.

"I know," thought Cherry brightly. "He's trying to glide down. A pancake landing, they call it. But oh, dear! In these trees too. Funny, but for once nobody, *absolutely nobody*, wants trees."

Then she thought how funny and clever she was to be thinking that way just now.

"It will be anytime now, Peter," she said softly and resting her cheek on top of his head she closed her eyes. Anytime, and *anything*, of course.

Stephen, head bent, came through from the cockpit. He had to keep his balance by holding the rack with one hand. Against slope and wobble he fought his way down the small plane.

"Give me Peter," he said, standing over Cherry, his voice controlled but urgent.

Cherry shook her head.

"He goes with me," she said.

To safety or eternity?

Stephen bent over her.

"You little fool," he said between closed teeth as he lurched over them, then saved himself by catching the back of the seat.

He seemed to loom over Cherry and the child.

"Strap yourself in, Stephen," Cherry said furiously. "What will become of us if *we* live and you're killed."

There was an awful second when Stephen's eyes met hers and it looked as if they'd spend their last precious seconds of life defying one another.

The thought must have occurred to Stephen for suddenly he righted himself, spun round in a half circle to sit in the empty seat behind Cherry.

He had just buckled his belt when the plane hit the top of the trees and swooped along them, cutting the leaf twigs and sapling branches in a swathe.

The plane lurched sideways, bumping badly as it made several minor hits on the branch tops. There were trees around and below them.

There was a dreadful moment of quivering silence, then the plane righted itself on top of a tree. A minute later, with a tearing breaking sound of tree-wood below them, it rolled over sideways, tipping its nose downwards.

Inside the plane there was now silence. Nearly a minute of time was lost before anyone realised they had stopped completely and the plane, hanging sideways, nose down, was balancing on a brace of trees.

CHAPTER SEVEN

Stephen pressed the safety button and flung off his belt, at the same moment the pilot came out of the cockpit.

Cherry didn't know what happened in the next few minutes. The pilot was struggling with her belt and Stephen with Tracy's belt. They were all on top of one another because of the tilted angle of the plane. Cherry when she stood up had to balance one foot on the side arm of a seat then climb her way out of the plane like a monkey.

Someone; Stephen, she thought; had wrung Peter from her arms.

A branch of the tree helped Cherry to climb out of the plane and she crawled along the branch to the fork of the main trunk. It was the biggest tree-trunk she had ever seen, slippery and green, with some kind of fungus growing over it. She slid down the trunk to the ground.

She was cut and badly bruised from the tree fall but she did not have time to think about it. Picking her way over and through enormous bushes, entangled with creeper, she came under the open door of the plane which was now above her like a manhole in the plane which was sideways down.

Stephen, lying down, was dangling Peter by the arms. "You'll have to catch him," he said peremptorily.

"I will," said Cherry.

And she knew she would. It was a long drop, but Cherry would catch him.

"Coming."

"Ready."

Stephen let his hands slide from under Peter's armpits and held the child a minute by the hands. Then he let go.

The judgement of drop and catch was a fraction of an inch out so Cherry had to lean backwards, a trifle off balance, for Peter to fall safely into her arms. He came like a thud of ton weight on to her chest and she fell backwards into the undergrowth of dry stick bush and creeper, but holding Peter above her.

Peter, for the first time, let out a passionate shriek of pain and rage. The cause was, however, no more than a sharp stick that had glanced down his cheek.

Cherry, by her backward fall, had added cuts and perforations to scratches but she was too occupied with what she had now to do even to notice them.

Tracy was crawling along the tree-trunk as she herself had done and then Stephen and the pilot swung themselves out of the plane, landing far below them in the bushes. As Cherry picked her way, with Peter in her arms, through the bushes, over fallen tree-trunks, green and mossed with age, round huge creeper-infested trees, she had no time to see if the men had broken anything and were lying there incapacitated below a plane that might any moment blow up. Petrol, she knew by the smell, was pouring everywhere.

She had one clear duty, and that was to see that Peter was safe.

She struggled on through the almost impenetrable bush, not once looking behind to see how anyone fared. She was at least six hundred yards away when she stumbled into a small clearing. By this time she was aware of Peter's weight; reaction from her own scramble to safety took control of her. She sank on the ground, still holding the child, exhausted and very near tears.

Peter, vigorously protesting against the grasp she had on him, brought her back to reality. She set the little boy down on the ground and stood up and turned round. She could see the top of Tracy's head coming in her direction through the jungle undergrowth.

"Heavens, did I come through that?" thought Cherry.

The bush around the clearing was like an impenetrable wall. Only the madness of desperation could have brought anyone through it. Peter, except for some scratches on his arms and legs, was safe in wind and limb. She herself was torn, scarred and smeared with green stains and black streaks from twigs and bark that had once seen and felt bushfire. Her hair would, of course, be all over the place but she had no interest in it. She was anxiously watching for signs that Stephen and Alan Donnelly were getting a safe distance away from the plane.

What if one or both had broken a leg, or something, in their drop from the tree-hung plane?

Tracy broke through the bushes into the clearing.

"Of course I've ruined my slacks," she said.

Cherry was torn between admiration for Tracy's casualness and a hysterical inclination to laugh. She would think about Tracy and what was, after all, a form of controlled bravery, later.

"Will you mind Peter if I go back and see if the men are all right?"

"They are," said Tracy. "I could hear them breaking through the bushes behind me. And swearing."

Tracy sat down on the dried leaves in the clearing and took a comb from the hip pocket of her slacks and meticulously did her hair.

"One likes to look respectable, even in the middle of a jungle," she said.

"I didn't even know we had jungle in this part of the north," said Cherry weakly.

She drew Peter to her and looked earnestly down into

70

his face to see how much or little he was suffering from this terrible adventure.

For once Peter was not interested in Cherry. He gazed round in wonder and curiosity at his strange surroundings, then put two fingers in his mouth and began to suck them reflectively. He was mentally digesting this new experience.

Cherry felt inclined to be tearful at his philosophic resignation at the turn of events but she knew that Tracy would scorn her for any display of weakness. Tracy's posing had become a welded part of her nature so that she not only appeared to feel undisturbed, Cherry was inclined to believe she actually was undisturbed.

The two men broke through the wall of bush. Beneath the scratches, bruises and general dishevelment they were unharmed.

Stephen looked first at Peter then herself.

"Peter all right?" he asked.

"A hundred per cent," said Cherry.

"And you?" Without waiting for a reply he turned to the other. "You all right, Tracy?"

Tracy put the back of her comb between her teeth while she pressed shape into her hair with her fingers. She nodded.

Suddenly Stephen smiled.

"A hundred out of a hundred to you, Tracy," he said. "You'd never have hysterics, that's for sure."

Cherry felt a little dashed. After all, she hadn't had hysterics either. But then she was only the governess and governesses never had hysterics and never let their charges have them either. Nor nursemaids, for that matter.

Alan Donnelly sat back on his heels and reached in the pocket of his shirt for cigarettes. He held up the packet first to Tracy then Stephen.

"We'll smoke mine first," he said. "We might need yours to-morrow. We'll give the bus five minutes to blow up and if she doesn't we'll go back and salvage the gun. We'll all need to eat."

He looked across the clearing at Cherry.

"You made a nice save of that youngster, Miss Landin.

Thank you for behaving so well; and apologies for landing you on the wrong airstrip."

Cherry's heart warmed to Alan because she saw that under his carefully casual comments he understood himself to be responsible for their predicament.

" I think a thunderbolt is an Act of God," she said brightly. " I know my mother and father could insure their house against everything, except an Act of God. The company said that was something outside human safeguard."

Alan Donnelly gave her a rueful smile across the distance.

" We'll see what our insurance company says about the plane," he said. " Maybe *they'll* think it was a matter of human judgment – flying into that cloud."

Stephen was the only one not sitting. He had taken a cigarette and stood smoking it, looking into the bush beyond which that plane lay straddling a brace of giant trees. If it blew up, they were indeed in a predicament.

Tracy lay back on the leafy ground, her hands under her head. She stretched her legs and arched her insteps, so that her toes pointed – a favourite exercise when she was otherwise relaxing.

Stephen turned his head and glanced at her. Once again he allowed himself a smile.

Cherry wished she herself could feel as irresponsible as Tracy looked this very moment. Having achieved safety, Cherry now thought of something else. Peter would need food more urgently than any of them. And water too.

An hour later it was clear the plane would not blow up though a little earlier it had settled down into the trees with a terrible crash. This latter made foraging raids easier.

Stephen was the natural leader for he knew and understood the bush and Alan Donnelly did not.

Cherry had always been intrigued by the strange quality both Hugh and Stephen Denton had of being easy and measured in their movements one minute, and the next being able to act with great pace and authority.

It was Stephen of the two men now who went into action at top speed. With an almost unnatural strength and no wasting of time in explanations he proceeded to cut some sort of a path from the clearing through to the plane wreckage. From the emergency hatch of the plane he first retrieved a hatchet, the gun and cartridges and a portable tool box.

He directed and Alan co-operated. Tracy too came in for her share of work for Stephen did not hesitate to give her orders now. She was handed, small loads at a time, such things as the airline company's rugs, the linen covers from the seats, small packages of food such as biscuits, tea, and instant coffee. Two tins of dried milk had most blessedly been found for Peter.

Meantime Cherry was detailed off to mind Peter and at the same time to dig down into the roots of a nearby tree where Stephen hazarded an informed guess they might find water.

Cherry had never dug at depth before, much less with the small spade they found amongst the plane's emergency gear. It was hard going and dirty work but she dug with a will.

As soon as the first supplies arrived at the clearing Stephen had ordered that Peter be fed with some of the biscuits, and a little lemonade found amongst the plane's food supplies. He was then put to sleep on the bundle of rugs.

Then Cherry had to get on with her digging.

By the time the men had salvaged the essentials from the plane, and cut an easier path through the stretch of jungle, Cherry had dug deep enough to discover the earth was very moist around the roots of the tree Stephen had selected as the water indicator.

"Good!" Stephen said, smiling encouragingly as Cherry emerged from the hole with this news.

She guessed she was a fearful sight for this dank earth here amongst the trees was black, and heavy with rotten tree droppings and fungus from the surface roots. Her wayward hair kept falling forward across her brow into her eyes. Constantly lifting her hand to brush it back had left wood and earth stains on her face. And there was no clear water to wash in.

Her slacks, she decided, would never come clean again.

73

Both girls were grateful that Stephen had seen that their clothes were rescued from the plane.

Later when Stephen obliged by giving them a ten-minute break from the chores, Cherry, though beginning to feel very exhausted, thought she would slip into the trees and change those slacks. A blouse too if she dared such an extravagance at this stage. So far no ten minutes had been allowed.

It was nearly sundown when Stephen called a halt to labours.

After Cherry's discovery of very moist earth in the water-hole Stephen had taken the spade and deepened and widened the hole so that it now stood at about five foot depth. At the bottom, water began to seep into it.

The food was rationed at sundown. Dried milk and biscuits for Peter; one biscuit and a bar of chocolate each with a good strong cup of instant coffee for the others. The plastic cups and plates used on the plane had all been brought to the clearing.

Throughout this hard day's work, very little had been said by anyone. All had worked quickly and in near silence.

Alan had said that he was reasonably certain the plane would not catch fire at this stage but they had to guard against eventualities. The petrol tanks had burst and the petrol poured everywhere. It was evaporating fast but was obviously a danger until time or a heavy rainfall had rendered it ineffective. Hence the pace at which the essentials for camp life had to be retrieved from the plane.

Alan further expressed the opinion that the wreckage could not now be seen from the air. It had settled right down into the trees.

Stephen, even after hours of hard manual work, was still indefatigable in his labours at sundown. He built a small camp-fire in the middle of the clearing while Alan went back to the plane to see if there was any chance of repairing the wireless contacts.

It wasn't till dark, when Peter was finally put to bed for the night in a low-hanging hammock made from one of the rugs, that they all sat down round the fire and had

74

time to take stock of what had been done and what they might do on the morrow.

Through the flickering firelight Cherry could see Stephen's partly shadowed face, thoughtful but seemingly unconcerned.

"Sorry you're all on short rations to-night," he said over the cups of coffee. Water had been taken cup by cup from the hole and boiled and strained into one of the tins that had held dried milk. The former contents had been carefully packaged in a plastic bag that had held biscuits.

Stephen drew the gun towards him, and rested his hand on it.

"To-morrow, we'll hunt," he said. He looked at Tracy. "How about it?" It was an invitation with a smile and once again Cherry admired him for his capacity to turn this into something of a pleasure instead of what it was, sheer necessity.

Tracy nodded languorously. She had been working hard carrying things from the plane and this she was not used to doing. All her energy when on the station had been directed towards improving her muscle control when dancing.

"Long as I don't have to cut another path through that jungle; or swing from tree to tree like the monkeys," she said.

"We don't have any monkeys in Australia," Stephen said equably. "Pity. They would have been useful."

"For eating?" asked Tracy, wrinkling up her nose.

"Better than nothing," said Stephen dryly. "But to get on with plans for to-morrow. I think we'll operate in pairs. Keep that as an inviolable rule, will you?" This last he addressed to them all. "Tracy and I understand the bush better than you and Cherry, Alan. I think I'll make you camp commissariat officer. Cherry will have her hands full with Peter. By the way, he must not be left for an instant. You understand that, Cherry?"

She agreed. As if it was necessary to tell her! But then, that was like Stephen.

"You can fill in your spare time getting as much water as possible. Keep the fire going and boil the water as you get it. It probably won't be more than a pint at a time."

Cherry nodded.

He paused, then added:

"If anyone has cigarettes, aspirins or tablets of any kind, chocolates, et cetera, it is necessary to pool them. I think you all understand why. That way we can share them equally."

Alan drew a packet of cigarettes from his pocket and tossed it across the space to Stephen.

"Here it comes," he said. "I think you got that half carton we found in the plane earlier?"

Stephen nodded.

"Any booty, Cherry?" he asked her.

"A small packet of barley-sugar in my handbag," she said.

She went to the place near the tree fringe where the girls had been given some rugs to make a private dressing-room. She came back with her handbag, opened it and took out the packet. She held it out to Tracy to pass to Stephen.

The packet had been opened before the plane crashed and Tracy now helped herself to a square of barley-sugar then passed the packet on.

She arched her eyebrows and looked slightly superior as she did this.

"Payment for a hard day's work," she said.

Stephen smiled.

"In that case I think we'll have one each all round. We've all worked hard."

The barley-sugar was handed round.

Tracy made no contribution on the grounds she never had headaches and so never carried aspirin. She said nothing of cigarettes.

Stephen, getting up lazily from the fire, added the barley-sugar to the other booty in the fork of a tree.

"I'll do the rationing," he said equably as he came back to the fire. "Alan, you stand guard during my absence. Right?"

Everyone nodded.

"How dishonest do you think we all are?" Tracy said haughtily.

76

"Not at all," said Stephen. "Everyone knows where the store is kept but if we're some time in being rescued we'd be foolish to expend our luxuries unwisely. I think we all deserve one more break to-night. Alan, here comes your packet of cigarettes. Hand them round, will you?"

Cherry was the only one who didn't smoke so she shook her head.

"Go ahead. Have one," Alan Donnelly said with a grin. "To-night is a luxury and a treat. You might as well join in."

"No thank you," said Cherry again. "Not that I wouldn't like to join in but that would be a tragic waste. In a day or two someone might wish they had the cigarette I'd smoked to-night."

Alan had not unwrapped his piece of barley-sugar. He leaned over to pass it to her.

"Then you take this," he insisted.

Again Cherry shook her head.

"You'll need that for energy," she said. "It's not a treat, it's almost medicine when one gets tired and there's not too much in the stomach."

"Quite right," said Stephen. "We'll find some other way of giving Cherry a treat to-morrow." He changed the subject brusquely. "Is everyone clear about to-morrow? Tracy! Sun-up and you come hunting with me? Right?"

Tracy nodded.

"You shoot, I'll retrieve," she said calmly. "That is, if I can retrieve in that bush."

"And you two stick together," Stephen said finally to Cherry and Alan. "Don't get out of sight of one another. Tracy and I will do the same. To be lost in this jungle could be fatal."

Towards sundown on the second day Alan Donnelly took two of the linen seat covers and with the help of some splay pins from the plane's tool-box began to make a shoulder bag in which Peter might be carried.

"Are you married that you know about such things?" Cherry asked. They had become very companionable in their segregation together. Cherry liked the air-pilot very much. He was pleasant and amusing, full of droll stories about different people he met between flights in outback towns and stations. Cherry noticed they were mostly girls he talked about.

He shook his head to her question.

"No, but I made a carrying-seat from canvas for my sister who is married," he said, then added with a laugh, "The advantages of being an uncle, but also a bachelor."

Cherry, her hands black with damp earth and decayed leaf droppings, pushed the hair back from her eyes. She had been down the water-hole, pressing for more water.

"If only that other uncle," she said, meaning Stephen, "would find a creek or something. I'm afraid we rather tussle over Peter. Stephen watches me all the time to see I'm doing the right thing for his nephew but his greatest service would be to find good clear water." She paused and looked at Alan anxiously. "Do you suppose this dirty-looking water might make Peter ill?" she asked.

"It's not dirty when it's strained and boiled," he said. Then he looked up. "We'll have to move on, Cherry, I suppose you realise that? No plane has been heard or seen, which means we're well off the course. That struggle down there in that hole doesn't really provide quite enough for us all."

"That's what I was thinking," said Cherry soberly. "I daren't even wash my hands. And the food too. There's not much meat on those birds, is there?"

"Stephen says the aborigines live well enough on them."

"I suppose the jungle is too thick for him to catch a kangaroo or wild buffalo?"

"Stephen thinks that too, and he can't explore far. It takes too long cutting a path and he can't afford to get lost."

"No," agreed Cherry. "None of us can afford to get lost from one another, can we?"

Alan Donnelly lifted up his linen carrying-bag.

"Hence the doings," he said triumphantly, showing his finished article with pride. "Now someone can carry Peter comfortably."

Cherry smiled.

"You're very kind," she said, then added thoughtfully, "I don't think you quite ate your share of bird soup last night."

Alan shrugged.

"When you've been responsible for a plane crash," he said, "you kind of go off your food."

"Don't say that again," said Cherry firmly. "Besides——"

"Besides what?"

He was sitting on the ground cross-legged, putting finishing touches to his carrying-bag. Cherry came towards him, knelt down beside him and touched the work he was doing.

"We are having fun, aren't we?" she said lightly. "It's quite an adventure. I wouldn't even be worrying if it weren't for all the relatives."

Alan dropped his work and took her soiled hand, turned it palm up and looked at it.

"Call that fun?" he said. "You're not the kind that likes dirty hands, Cherry."

"But we're all the same," she laughed. "We're all dirty. It is rather fun."

"All except Tracy," said Alan, still holding her hand. "You're the gamest of us all, young Cherry. I can tell." He grinned. "I know a lot about girls."

"Oh no," said Cherry. "We're all the same——" She withdrew her hand reluctantly because somehow there was something of warmth in this close companionship.

"Two men can look after themselves, especially if one of them is a bushman like Stephen. And Tracy will always see she is looked after. There are tremendous advantages in being an artist like Tracy. She has to be looked after," Alan said.

"But she was awfully brave before the plane crashed. She just looked bored as if nothing worse was going to happen than a five-foot jump."

"And what were you? Scared?"

"I suppose I was, but I had young Peter. I couldn't

79

show it, you know. That's terribly bad for young children. They must never see adults frightened."

Alan smiled at her; at the same time his eyebrows flickered whimsically.

"Stephen was right," he said. "You're a good mother to Peter."

Cherry rose to her feet.

"I didn't think Stephen thought of me at all," she said.

"Stephen?" said Alan. "Heaven only knows what he thinks about any of us except he's rather impressed with the casual way Tracy takes everything. Imagine if we had two sick or hysterical women on our hands! No, he just happened to mention that a casual observer would think Peter belonged to you. Don't be angry about it, Cherry. It is only natural he should feel concerned about his brother's child."

"Of course. I quite agree. But I manage Peter much more capably than Stephen would."

"I think that's what he means."

Cherry busied herself wiping the damp earth and leaf-mould from her hands and arms. After a minute she looked across the short space between them and gave Alan an apologetic smile.

"I'm sorry I was touchy," she said. "It was silly of me."

"Quite understandable," said Alan evenly. "In a situation like this we're all apt to get a bit edgy."

"It's very nearly fun," said Cherry thoughtfully. "I said that before, didn't I?"

"If we didn't have the responsibility of a small child with us, and if we could let the outside world know where we are," agreed Alan. "Two men with two attractive girls ——" He laughed again.

After a long pause he looked up, and their eyes met. Cherry dropped her eyes and went on, more rapidly, cleaning her hands and arms with bunches of green leaf tips rolled into balls.

Peter at that moment was stirring in his hammock made of an airline rug. Cherry went over to him and lifted him out. She held him up in the air and smiled up into his face.

"Wake up, sleepy-head, there's more bird soup waiting for you. And Stephen said I might, I just might, give you one more biscuit with it."

Stephen and his eking out of the biscuits! Did he think she didn't know how to ration them herself?

"Darling Peter, I feel cross with your uncle," she whispered into his hair as she lowered him into her arms and carried him to a crèche they had made by dragging four logs together into a square. She set Peter down on the ground in his safety yard. "But don't tell him," she added. "We can't afford to quarrel until we get back to civilisation."

Could she afford to quarrel with him then, she wondered. After all, he was the brother of her employer. He was a part owner in the station where she earned her livelihood.

Peter was still too sleepy to be impressed by Cherry's reflections, even if he understood them. He sat comfortably on his nice padded seat, put two fingers in his mouth and regarded Cherry with lazy eyes. Cherry bent over and kissed him.

"Nobody ought dare quarrel over you, ragamuffin," she said. This was aloud and she was suddenly aware of Alan Donnelly watching her out of quizzical eyes.

Cherry flushed and turned away quickly to retrieve Peter's bird soup from the embers of the fire. She had been caught at playing being motherly again.

She wondered why, as she presently fed Peter, this should worry her. It was like exposing some deep secret of her nature and no one, she supposed, liked their inner self being exposed to the onlooking world. For some extraordinary reason it seemed to establish some unspoken bond between herself and Alan. It was too silly a thought, but really, spending the day in the camp like this, with the baby between them, made them look like a staid married couple.

Cherry was furious at the thought. The one thing she didn't want to be was "staid." She wanted to be young and gay – and, yes, modern like Tracy. And were Tracy and Stephen out there in the jungle looking like a staid married couple? Well, not Tracy, that was for sure. Nor Stephen either when you came to think of it. There were occasions when he was amused in a manner no one, but no one, could call *staid*.

One thing she was certain about – Alan wouldn't be dull taking a girl out. There were moments when he had a slightly devil-may-care light in his eyes when he told his stories of people – mostly girls – met on overnight stays on pilot duty.

CHAPTER EIGHT

Cherry had scarcely finished feeding Peter when Tracy came through the thick undergrowth into the clearing.

"Goodness, how does she do it?" thought Cherry.

Tracy's slacks were as stained and jagged as her own – she was reserving the two pairs salvaged in her bag from the plane for civilisation, Tracy said – but her hair, glowing like deep coals in the shadows of the trees, was smooth and beautiful as ever.

Cherry was suddenly and excitedly aware of something else about Tracy. Apart from the addition of a slightly smug look, Tracy's face was shining clean. So were her hands.

"Ducks for dinner," Tracy said, still in that slightly bored voice. "Stephen is de-feathering them now."

"Ducks?" said Cherry, hardly daring to hope. "Ducks swim on water. And your hands are clean."

"And so is the rest of me," said Tracy. "I've been swimming."

Alan had gone back to the plane wreckage for more salvage so Cherry was Tracy's only audience as she let herself sink to the ground in a single graceful movement.

"That," said Tracy, "calls for a cigarette."

She reached into her blouse pocket and pulled out a packet of cigarettes. She leaned forward and lifted a charred stick from the fire embers and held its coal to the end of her cigarette. Cherry ignored the surprise appearance of cigarettes.

"Forgive my interrupting you in that activity of yours, Tracy," said Cherry, standing holding Peter in her arms, "but if you've been swimming it's just possible you might tell me where. Then I could give Peter a bath."

"Yourself too," said Tracy, idly looking Cherry up and down. "Just how you got yourself in that mess – up to your armpits with mud, I guess – I'll never know."

"I don't suppose you will, but I'll give you an even break at finding out. I've been digging for water. Over there, in that hole. And the sand happens to be black when you get that far down."

"Quaint," said Tracy. "And I've never seen anything else but red earth up in these regions."

"Tracy, I'll shake you in a minute. Please, *please*. Where is the kind of water that can get you as clean as you look."

"I can hear Stephen coming through the bush. Ask him. He found it," said Tracy, expelling long shafts of smoke from her cigarette.

Stephen, carrying two brace of plucked ducks, broke through the heavy undergrowth. For a moment he stood on the outer edge of the clearing and looked at the two girls. Tracy was reclining comfortably on the ground, her face clean and her hair immaculate. Cherry, by this time standing near her, Peter still in her arms, was dishevelled with the evidence of her more recent wresting of water from the ground-hole very much on her face, hands and arms. It went without saying, Cherry thought, not without a touch of bitterness, that her hair was all over the place too.

Stephen looked as beautifully clean as Tracy did. While she and Peter, not to mention Alan Donnelly——

"If you two could bear to divulge your secret," Cherry said severely, "I might just be able to wash Peter before sundown."

Stephen walked into the centre of the clearing and threw the ducks on to the ground.

"Dinner," he said, with an air of triumph. "While Tracy

cooks them I'll take you and Peter to the great find of the century, Cherry."

Alan Donnelly could be heard coming back from the plane.

"And Alan too," said Cherry. "I guess he wouldn't mind washing his hands for dinner——"

Alan broke through the bushes. It took him a full minute to realise the change in Stephen and Tracy, and to see the ducks lying on the ground.

"You didn't find a station homestead too?" he asked with a delighted grin.

"No such luck," said Stephen. "But let's all be clean first and then we can talk about the day's luck in hunting. We found the edge of the jungle anyway. There's plains . . . open wide dusty plains about four miles due south."

"And hills in the distance, if you like a full description of the scenery," said Tracy. "The main thing is——"

"The main thing is," said Alan, giving a whoop of delight, "out on the plain a searching aircraft could spot us."

"Exactly," said Stephen. "But don't forget we can't go too far from our water find. It's about eight degrees north-west of the opening into the plain country."

"Please," pleaded Cherry, "could we go and bathe? I can't think of anything in the world more wonderful than clean water in large quantities."

"Of course," said Stephen. He strode over and took Peter from her arms. "On your way to the next thing to godliness, young feller," he said, addressing the child.

Peter twisted himself in Stephen's arms and looked over his shoulder at Cherry. He made the kind of demanding noises that meant he ought to be carried by Cherry.

"We've got a carrying-seat for him," said Cherry. "Alan's made it."

"It's not that far," said Stephen. "I'm quite capable of carrying my own nephew."

"What shall we do for towels?" asked Cherry, picking her way over the ground towards Stephen and Peter who were already turning towards the bush. She thought this was not the right moment to quarrel over Peter. If only the small darling wouldn't peer over Stephen's shoulder like that as if afraid she wasn't coming.

"What we did," said Tracy, still recumbent. "Nothing. And by the way I can't cook ducks."

Stephen paused.

"Then put Alan on the job," he said. "He's got quite a long wait."

"Oh no," protested Cherry. "He wants a wash and, much more, he wants a long, long drink too."

"Sorry," said Stephen. "We keep the party evenly divided. First rule of the bush. Never leave one alone. Two or more, yes. But not one."

"It's okay, Cherry," said Alan with a grin. "I'm going to give myself one nip of that brandy with some boiled dirty water as a toast to my later ablutions. But be a sweetheart — just don't be too long. Tracy, where have you been harbouring those illicit cigarettes?"

They were still mildly wrangling over cigarettes, and how to cook ducks, as Stephen and Cherry drowned the sound of their words with their own crashing and struggling through the heavy growth.

Cherry too had wondered where Tracy had got her packet of cigarettes. It had been agreed that all treasures be pooled and be rationed out only when all members of the party were present to share. Tracy must have kept her own treasure trove and said nothing about it. Oh well, she would be forgiven. Anyone as attractive and as stubbornly dependent and useless as was Tracy would be forgiven anything. Such people always were, Cherry reflected.

All the same, she still admired Tracy for not panicking in that plane, and not having hysterics or making complaints since. Cherry quite overlooked that she herself hadn't offended in any of these categories either.

She followed Stephen through the heavy jungle undergrowth. Now and again Peter gave a cry of protest as some prickly bush or branch-end whipped across his arms or legs. Stephen kept Peter's face shielded with his hand.

Already, from conversation the night before, Cherry knew how Stephen could follow his own tracks through the jungle.

He followed the natives' device of breaking the twig ends of branches as he went along. It made exploring slower but certainly safer.

He was now following his own trail of broken branches. Presently, though there was still little light through the dense growth, Cherry knew they were going down an incline. She had a tendency to slip on the damp carpet of dead leaves.

Quite suddenly there was light through the trees. Then suddenly they stood on the edge of rocks. Below them was a still pool of water in a round basin, about fifteen feet across. There were lilies growing on the far edge and half a dozen birds gliding over its surface.

" Oh ! " gasped Cherry, then asked, " Is it safe to drink?"

" If it weren't there'd be dead stuff around, the remains of reptiles and birds. And I've never heard of ducks swimming on poisoned water."

" Of course," said Cherry. " I suppose that was a stupid question to ask. But the birds do swim on heavily-salted water, don't they?"

" I took the precaution of watching the birds, first," Stephen said dryly. " And Tracy and I have drunk long and deep. I feel perfectly fit."

For a moment Cherry thought he might be reproaching her for looking a gift horse in the mouth, or worse, cowardice.

" I was thinking of Peter," she said gravely.

Stephen looked over Peter's head. His eyes smiled.

"So was I," he said.

Cherry flushed. It was as if she had been caught out assuming he thought of her.

" How do we get down?" Cherry asked in order to banish every thought except those that dealt with the miracle of wide waters and swimming birds.

Stephen, still carrying Peter, began to pick his way down over the stony shore of the small lake.

" There just could be fish down there," said Cherry conversationally as she followed him. This was a glad moment, she felt, and she ought to make it sound glad.

" If we had time to fish," said Stephen's voice, muffled by

the fact he did not look round and Peter's body as well as his own shoulder intervened.

They reached the bottom of the short, boulder-strewn incline and Stephen stooped and put Peter down. The child gazed at the water in absorbed interest. He put out his hands towards it.

" I'll wash him first," said Cherry.

" I'll do that," said Stephen. " If you just go along about a hundred yards you can bathe yourself."

There was no shelter or privacy around the entire shore of that strange lake. One could climb up among the boulders, Cherry thought, but then one would still have to descend over an open space into the water.

Even if she swam in her underclothes . . .! But she would like to wash them!

" Well, spring to it," said Stephen with a half-angry unevenness in his voice. " You will excuse Peter and me being absorbed in other things."

Once again Cherry flushed for she realised Stephen understood her predicament and he was curtly telling her that bathing in their peculiar circumstances was more important than prudery.

He had rolled up the legs of his trousers, turned his back on the northern portion of the shore to which he had directed Cherry and bending over Peter began to divest the child of his clothing.

Peter was not only amenable, he was delighted.

" Water, water!" he seemed to crow. " Just let me in to splash!"

Cherry picked her way along the beach, took off her clothing and slipped into the water.

It was sheer delight to her hot moist body. Suddenly she didn't care any more about the man and the child farther along the lakeside.

Cold water! Clear cold water and rounded stones for a lake bottom. Oh . . . what wonderful heaven!

She bent down to scoop between the stones and bring up sufficient quartz-like sand with which to rub herself all over.

"Very abrasive form of soap," she reflected. "But, oh, how wonderful, wonderful!"

She turned over on her back and floated.

All around the lake was a wall of jungle bush and trees, straight overhead was the grey circle of humid sky. If there was any sun shining Cherry did not see it but that sky was so light the sun must be somewhere in the universe. It certainly dealt out its heat if not its rays into this choking jungle.

Suddenly across that space of open sky there came two wedge-shaped lines like the chevrons on a soldier's sleeve.

"Birds," she thought. "More birds, and not ducks."

The lines came closer, circled the opening above the lake and then breaking their formation came down, down, down to the water.

"*Pelicans!*" Cherry cried aloud.

She crouched down in the water, her face turned up, and watched.

They came in flocks now.

After the pelicans came what she thought were herons and ibis. Then ducks and ducks and ducks. There were brown and black and grey ducks, small ones, big ones . . . and yes, *swans*. Then flying in, in a small covey, came seagulls.

Cherry wiped the water out of her eyes as if wiping away magic mists.

"I don't believe it," she said. "*Seagulls!* We must be five hundred miles inland."

Suddenly the whole lake was covered with feathers. In a minute the birds would crowd her out of the water altogether.

In her wonder and excitement she nearly called out to Stephen but remembered in time she was handicapped by an absence of clothes.

She had brought her underclothes to the edge and realising that the homecoming of birds must mean the near approach of sundown, she retrieved the clothes and did her best, while sitting deep in water, to wash them.

All the time, along the beach, Stephen appeared to take

no interest in anything but Peter's joyous splashing in the water.

"Oh, I must hurry," thought Cherry remorsefully. "He's got to take us back, and then bring Alan."

At the thought of Alan waiting in the steaming camp clearing for a share in that heaven she herself was enjoying, she wrung out her clothes, hastened back on to the water's edge and drew them on over her damp body.

She hadn't thought to bring a comb for her hair – Tracy would sooner have parted with life than her comb.

She pulled on her rubber-soled shoes and ran along the beach to Stephen.

"Isn't it wonderful?" she cried excitedly. "Stephen! Look at the birds. There must be millions of them. Where did they come from?"

Hearing her voice Stephen straightened up and turned round. He did not look at Cherry. He stood looking across the lake where one could see only small patches of water between the flocks of birds.

Even as they watched, red-legged hens came out of the water and began to run over the stony ground, hunting with their beaks for grubs they appeared to find in plenty.

"That is how the natives learn to find food," Stephen said casually. "By watching the birds."

"And the natives eat grubs, of course."

"Yes. I'm thankful we haven't had to resort to it ourselves. Well, come along, we'd better get back. Alan will be parched out with waiting."

He stopped and picked up Peter. On the beach he sat back on his heels trying to get Peter's clothes on without fumbling.

"Give him to me," said Cherry, reaching forward for the child.

For a moment it looked as if Stephen would protest, but it was clear, even to him, that there was a mystery about a child's clothes and a further mystery as to how to get them on over a wet body.

He surrendered Peter to Cherry who immediately demonstrated that the mystery was no more than the know-how married to experience.

"Very clever," Stephen observed. "And quick too."

"I'm being quick on purpose," Cherry said, finishing Peter up to his linen hat. "I stayed too long in the water and it might be sundown before Alan gets here." She looked up at Stephen anxiously. "He would never find his way back in the dark, would he? I mean, you'll come with him, won't you?"

Stephen stood up. Cherry was now holding the wriggling Peter in her arms and Stephen put out his hands to take the child.

"I'll carry him," said Cherry. "You've made this trip twice to-day already and you have to come back with Alan."

Stephen took Peter from Cherry without her permission.

"Don't be foolish," he said as he turned and began to climb up the rocky bank of the lake. "You can't climb and carry a heavy child. You might slip and then Peter would be injured."

Unburdened, Cherry sprang nimbly from rock to rock and now stood a few feet ahead of the man and child. She turned and looked at Stephen angrily.

"I would never injure Peter," she said. "And though you are quite right to worry about him first, it's not very chivalrous of you to fail to consider I might be injured too."

Stephen stood quite still and looked at the angry girl. He very nearly laughed. Cherry stood astride two boulders, her slacks were damp where she had drawn them on over her wet body. Her blouse clung to her firmly. Her hair, still wet, looked slightly more urchinish than usual.

It wasn't altogether the angry impish figure she cut standing there, so much as the lack of logic in her way of thinking, that brought forth that old tantalising half-smile of Stephen's.

"My dear child," he said, looking Cherry up and down and through. "One minute you insist you can carry Peter safely, the next minute you are indignant because there is no sympathy for such injuries as you yourself might sustain in a fall."

Cherry felt deflated. Moreover, she was suddenly physically

conscious of the odd figure she made. How unlike Tracy, he was undoubtedly thinking. Tracy came back to camp sparkling clean and every hair of her sophisticated head in place.

Cherry turned about and went on scrambling up the rocks.

"I'm sorry. I'm crabby," she said. "It's the excitement. And worry too. I'm afraid Alan won't get here in time."

"He will. I'll show him how to find the blazed trail and Tracy can take him through safely. I'll let them have the torch and two batteries in case sundown beats them."

Cherry stopped again.

"Aren't you going with him?" she asked anxiously.

"No. He's a grown man, and Tracy knows the way, approximately."

"But Tracy——"

Cherry had been going to say that Tracy would be incompetent in such a task but she knew one woman must never speak disparagingly of another woman to a man. Especially when the other woman had a special interest in that man.

"But Tracy," she finished lamely, "is going to cook the dinner."

"We'll attend to that if Alan hasn't done something about it already," Stephen said. Then after a few more steps upwards which now took them to the jungle edge, "In case you doubt Tracy's capacity to take care of Alan Donnelly in the bush you are underestimating her by a long distance. Tracy, in spite of her stage and ballet training, was reared on a station. On horseback, in a bullock muster and in the jungle, Tracy is quite superb."

"Oh . . ." said Cherry, then added to show she was sporting about another girl, "she was superb in the plane too. Before it crashed, I mean. It's just that, well, being a girl she mightn't want to make this trip twice."

"She won't kidnap Alan, if that is what you are afraid of."

Cherry flushed again. There was a tang to Stephen's words and she thought they meant to imply that Cherry herself had claims on Alan.

Cherry could have, that moment, in spite of her heavenly swim and all the wonderful adventure of the homing birds, cried with the frustration of being a woman. A girl can never satisfactorily answer a man back. Her dignity and her private loves were always at stake. Men like Stephen always got the better of one.

"In addition," said Stephen, plunging into the jungle a yard ahead of Cherry, "there is the inviolable rule – we work in mixed pairs. One man and one girl. That way lies safety when lost in the bush."

"Then I will come back with Alan," said Cherry impetuously.

"And neither of you really knowing the way? Just show me the way we should turn now after we work our way round this old cabbage tree."

Cherry looked about her. She would have given anything to catch sight of one or some of those broken twigs.

She had to give in.

"I don't know," she said helplessly.

"This time it's the ground you look at," said Stephen. "The ground is clearer under the tree so I simply kicked a sand path through the leaves."

"All right, you win," said Cherry. "I won't make any more suggestions."

"Tracy saw me making all the tracks," said Stephen in a placatory voice. Then suddenly his tone changed to one of teasing. "Besides, you would hardly leave Peter to my tender mercies, would you?"

"Only for some of the time," Cherry conceded.

They reached a point when they were pushing their way through thick vines, side by side.

She turned her head and caught Stephen looking at her again with that slightly ironic gleam in his grey eyes.

"What are you laughing at?" she asked. There was a hint of challenge in her own blue eyes. She ceased tearing apart the lower bushes while she turned to look into his face.

"You," he said. "So earnest, so incompetent when it comes to parting bushes without cutting yourself——"

"At least I'm trying——" said Cherry, indignant. She let the bush stems fall back, and pushed the hair out of her eyes with the back of a green-stained hand.

"Granted," said Stephen. "Now if you were Tracy you'd let me do it with my heavy boots, like this."

He had great and easy strength for he trod the bushes down at their bases so that they parted and leaned sideways, leaving a passage for the intruders to pass through.

"Like that!" he said, as if demonstrating something very simple to a child.

"If I were Tracy——" began Cherry, exasperated, then stopped.

"Well what?" asked Stephen over Peter's shoulder.

Cherry nearly tossed her head.

"I would own a station, and a beautiful town house by the ocean down south. And I would marry a tall, rich, ungallant stranger——"

"Why ungallant, and why a stranger?"

"Well, he wouldn't be those things to Tracy," conceded Cherry. "Please, Mr. Denton, if you wouldn't mind continuing on with those big boots of yours, I'll pretend – for the time being only, of course, that I'm Tracy. I'll follow where you lead."

"Good," said Stephen. "Now we'll be able to make better progress."

Cherry looked at Stephen's back as he preceded her through the scramble of trees.

She wished she could laugh, but somehow that was just what she couldn't do. She *wasn't* Tracy, and nothing she could do about it would alter that fact.

CHAPTER NINE

They went on their way back through the jungle in silence and truce. Cherry was sorry for her momentary pique because underneath her general crossness with Stephen she was admiring him very much. His bushcraft had been quite staggering and his resourcefulness unlimited. Moreover, in all fairness, she had to admit he was quite right to attach so much importance to his responsibility for the little boy.

"I'm getting too fond of Peter," Cherry thought. "I'm getting possessive. That would be fatal. I must do something about being objective."

Her toughest obstacle in achieving such an end was young Peter himself. He was so delighted with being fresh and clean, the joy of splashing in clear water was still with him. When they got back to the camp he held out his arms to Cherry and Stephen had willy-nilly to give him up. There were men's chores to be attended to and now was the moment when Cherry, nursemaid or governess, whichever she was, was paid to take over.

Alan had a good coal-fire going preparatory to cooking the ducks.

"On a spit? Or cover them with hot coals?" he asked Stephen. "We can't afford to spoil the dinner by the cooking."

"Leave it to me," said Stephen. "I'll give Cherry a lesson in bush cooking and after that she can take over as camp cook."

"Bit tough on Cherry," said Alan protectively. He glanced at Cherry and it was clear from the expression on his face he thought Cherry had her hands full with young Peter, and Stephen was asking too much.

"The rest of us are going to be busy other ways," Stephen said dryly.

Tracy came out from the rug camp, holding a bundle of clothes.

"I suppose I go with Alan?" she asked lightly. "Well, he can wash his own shirts, but, darling——" this was to Stephen, "I'll manage yours with pleasure, since you so cleverly found the water."

"Take the two canvas waterbags," said Stephen. "It might be pleasant to have more drinking water here too." He handed Alan the torch and added, "Light too, if you stay dallying with water too long."

When they had gone Stephen set about mixing some of the boiled water they had in hand with red earth from the edge of the clearing.

"It's like a paste," said Cherry, watching.

"That's exactly what it is."

He encased two of the birds with this clay paste so that not one part was left bare, then dug a shallow hole under the coals of Alan's fire. He placed the birds in the hole, put over them the last of the clay and then scraped back the coals for a topping.

"The earth under the fire is hot," he explained. The coals on top will keep it that way. Important thing is to keep a fine scraping of hot cinders on top. Otherwise you can forget them. They'll be cooked fine and succulent by the time the others return."

Cherry was impressed. She knew this was the manner in which the aborigines cooked their game but she had never seen it done and did not dream a white man would follow the example.

The short dusk and early night came down on the bush. The only light was from the flickering flames of the campfire. Stephen, Cherry and Peter were all tired from the day's excitement and activity.

Stephen said he refused to be worried because Tracy and Alan were not back from the lake.

"They had no chance of being back before early evening," he said. "If they miss the way, even with the torch, they'll sit down and wait till morning."

"But Stephen——"

He turned his head in the fireglow and looked at her. Cherry was sitting farther round the fire from him. Neither of them was very near it for it was a warm tropical night and they only needed the fire for light and for cooking.

"Nobody," he said tersely, "certainly neither you nor I, would have a chance of finding them in the dark. Don't forget they have the big torch. They're grown-up and sensible. They won't wander about in the bush at night either."

"It might be embarrassing for them," said Cherry out of Mr. and Mrs. Landin's old-fashioned background.

Stephen looked at her again. His voice held a mixture of surprise and annoyance.

"Beggars can't be choosers," he said, "and neither can two people lost in the bush choose their company." He stopped, then added, "For that matter you and Peter and I can hardly be held responsible for the company we're choosing right now."

"Of course," said Cherry, but she would have liked to pick up a broken piece of tree branch and throw it at him.

Anyway, it was only human to worry about the other two. Stephen didn't appear, on this subject, to have even the rudimentary virtues of the human heart.

They sat in silence for some while. Cherry did notice that Stephen did not give himself the treat of the evening cigarette. At least in that respect he had more generosity than Tracy who had kept her own private cache. Stephen was in charge of the pooled resources of the small camp and he might very easily now have taken his own share. He didn't do this and Cherry felt she had considerable respect for his discipline and his sense of honour on the point. He would wait until Alan Donnelly and Tracy were here to share, and by the pitch blackness of the bush all around them now, Cherry guessed it would be a long wait until morning.

A little later Stephen got up and retrieved the shotgun from its place along the lower branch of one of the bulky trees on the edge of the clearing.

"I'll send up a shot to let them know we've noticed their absence," he said.

He discharged one barrel into the air.

Peter, who was dozing, woke with a cry.

"I ought to feed Peter," Cherry said. She couldn't mention the fact that for a long time she had been wondering about those ducks under the embers, and every time she wondered her mouth watered. The thought of food made her more hungry than its relative absence had made her during the preceding two days.

"We'll crack one of the birds," Stephen said. "The other we can leave for breakfast."

He raked aside the embers and with a stout stick levered out of its bed one of the hard clay-encased ducks. He took

96

a sharp-edged stone to crack the case. It fell apart in two pieces. There, steaming, succulent, and emitting the most glorious smell, lay the perfect roasted duck.

"The aborigines do it with the feathers on," said Stephen, "but I spared you that."

Cherry brought one of the plates salvaged from the plane and Stephen tipped the duck on to it, carefully retaining the tiny residue of fat and meat juice in the bottom of the clay cup.

"That's for Peter," he said.

"But it's fatty," warned Cherry.

"But still very good for him. On this point I'm the best judge."

"But you don't know anything about children's stomachs. He's still a baby."

"So are the aborigines when they start taking this kind of soup."

Cherry in her anxiety to see that Peter was fed rightly had almost forgotten her own hunger.

"He can suck some of the bird flesh——" began Cherry.

"And spoon up this meat juice too. Fat and all. I never heard such a lot of nonsense as you women think and talk when it comes to a child short on the food ration and virtually lost in the bush. Does it occur to you Peter has probably lost a pound weight in the last fifty-six hours?"

This was unfair, for Cherry had given Peter most of her own bird soup as well as his own ration. He was the only one to have the powdered milk and the biscuits. She could say nothing of this, of course.

She wished she could give in gracefully to Stephen on the point but her judgment was all against the fatty meat juice and she had Peter's well-being at stake.

"He can have my share of duck," she said almost aggressively. "As a matter of fact I don't like duck anyway. I never did——"

Stephen was standing quite still above the gently smoking dinner. He looked through the firelight at Cherry. His silence made her nervous and therefore talkative.

"You know, when we have it for Christmas dinner sometimes, instead of turkey, I always have to pretend to eat it, and pretend to like it . . . for Mummy's sake. But really ____"

"Big children, as well as little children," said Stephen evenly, "will eat what's set before them when there's a food shortage. Hunger is a good healthy antidote to faddism."

Cherry flushed. The warmth and fire had dried out her clothes and she stood before him, the collar of her self-dried blouse sprouting out from under her chin like an angry frill. Her slacks, alas, had shrunk an inch or two; her vagabondish haircut – so badly in need of a trim – hung wispishly in her eyes. Her feet were firmly planted apart and Stephen had the illusion he was facing a small feminine tornado about to break loose.

He bent down and carefully put the clay bowl with its precious residue of meat juice on the ground, then straightening himself up he walked round the dish of roast duck and with quiet deliberation took Cherry's shoulders in his hands. Holding her firmly, he looked down into her face.

"People get a bit touchy in these situations," he said quietly.

Alan Donnelly had said that earlier in the day and for one deflated moment Cherry wondered if she was turning out to be one of those people who "*just couldn't take it.*"

Tracy's relaxed and apparent indifference to the oddness and the rigours of the experience were evidently the correct fronts to put on in these circumstances.

Cherry admired Tracy for that bored calmness. So, evidently, did Stephen and Alan.

"I'm sorry," said Cherry but her lips trembled and the words choked a little in her throat.

But it was about Peter she was worrying, not herself! She couldn't tell Stephen that, of course.

He gently but firmly turned her and indicated the comfortable sitting place she had been in earlier. Yesterday the men had dug with their heels these shallow ground hollows and put in them the seats out of the plane.

"Sit down and I'll bring you something to eat," he said

with a solicitude that made her grit her teeth. "You'll feel better."

"But it's Peter's eating time," Cherry protested as, since she was forced to do so, she had to sit down.

"Peter is asleep. He too can wait his turn."

Cherry drew her knees up under her and resting her elbows on them cupped her chin in her hands.

How badly had she behaved? she wondered. She hadn't actually said anything, had she? It must have been the way she looked. He was treating her like an invalid. Or worse, like a difficult relative that needed coddling in order to keep her quiet.

She suddenly had a new idea.

Could he, very cunningly, be getting his own way? By putting her out of action he was going to feed Peter with indigestible fat.

Cherry slewed her eyes round and peered through the fire-light at Stephen. He had broken the duck apart and was bringing her a portion on a plastic plate. He put it on the ground beside her and so doubtful was she of his intentions, and so humiliated by his "little troublesome girl" treatment of her that she did not say thank you.

A minute later he came back with another helping of duck on another plate. He sat down beside her.

"Now eat," he said. "I'll keep you company."

Cherry was not only hungry, she was *not* childish; and she was incapable of sulking. She picked up the plate and resting it on her knees took a piece of duck flesh in her fingers. When she put it to her mouth she thought she would die of the delight of real food, tasty, and well cooked.

Stephen, eating with relish himself, was watching her. Cherry turned her head guiltily and their eyes met. Stephen smiled. Then Cherry smiled back.

He lifted his hand and pulled the vagrant lock of her hair hanging across her temple.

"Not so bad, eh?" he said kindly.

Cherry shook her head, for there were suddenly tears blinding her eyes. Kindness often hurts more than hostile reproaches, but she could never let him know this. She had to pretend it was the smoke from the camp-fire getting in her eyes.

"You worry too much," he said presently, when they had finished their meal and wiped their greasy fingers on the ground leaves around them.

"Not really," said Cherry, nearly back to her old self. "Apart from Peter it seems rather unkind of us to be sitting here so safely and comfortably when the others are lost in the bush."

"They'll have their camp-fire too," said Stephen with an attempt at comforting her. "If Alan hasn't enough nous to wring the neck of one of those red-legged water-hens Tracy will tell him how to do it. Somewhere down there in the jungle they're doing just what we're doing. And waiting for morning."

"Oh!" said Cherry, deflated.

"And Tracy will not be trying to seduce Alan. Or vice versa, if that's what's worrying you. Tracy has her mind on other things, and I've a shrewd idea Alan has his mind on other people."

"Don't you think you're entitled to your nightly cigarette?" said Cherry to change the conversation."

"I'll have two to-morrow night instead, but don't shelve your worries that way, my dear child. Let's dispose of the current disposition of the plane crash survivors first. Then to feeding Peter and sleep afterwards."

"I don't quite understand——"

"Those two are as safe as if they were sitting in that front sitting-room of yours in the Street of the Pines, with Mrs. Landin for chaperone."

"Don't you laugh at my mother," said Cherry spiritedly.

"I'm not. I'm laughing at you. I trust you feel perfectly safe in my company, Cherry."

Now he was laughing, just as he had that day sitting talking to her mother in the home near the ocean.

"I couldn't imagine anything safer," she said coldly.

"You are safe, my child," said Stephen, getting up and

picking up the plates. "But not your reputation? Is that what you are thinking? I don't advise you to write and tell your parents about it all – when we do eventually get out of here."

Cherry was standing up too. Once again she was the small irate figure with the firelight flickering over her rumpled collar, half-mast slacks, and undisciplined hair fringe.

"Do you know what?" she said steadily and in concentrated fierce defence against Stephen's silent laughter at the expense of her home and her upbringing. "Do you know what? I hate you."

He paused in surprise, turned his head and looked at her. If ever there was a sweet tiger ready to spring, it was Cherry.

"I'm so sorry," said Stephen infuriatingly. Then walking away he added, without turning to see whether she heard him or not, "In the morning, after a good sleep, you'll feel different."

Cherry dug her fingernails into the palms of her hands. "I mustn't, I mustn't, I mustn't," she said between clenched teeth, fighting to keep silence and control of her anger. "He thinks I'm just a difficult woman, overwrought because I've been plane-wrecked and am scared I won't ever get found again. And Tracy is perfect at self-discipline."

Then she fell to wondering if just that was indeed what was wrong with her.

How dreadful! She had better try and become more like Tracy. And anyhow, she didn't feel the least bit afraid.

Lying in her bush bed, with the rug screen shielding both herself and the baby from the flickering firelight, she took herself to task again. She didn't feel afraid, and she knew why. It was Stephen's calm managership of the camp and his unlimited knowledge of the bush that made them all safe. Without him it all might have been a very different story.

Cherry put her hand over the edge of the hammock Alan Donnelly had made for Peter and felt the sleeping child's warm arm. Her hand slid gently up over his cheek and lightly stroked the downy head.

She felt comforted.

It was still dark when Stephen called Cherry back from a deep sleep.

He touched her on the shoulder and spoke gently so as not to wake Peter.

"Time to get up, Cherry," he said. "It will be daylight in an hour and I want to get some shooting done before the birds take off."

Cherry sprang up immediately.

"Yes," was her first thought, "and Tracy and Alan have to be found!" Stephen was probably just as anxious as she was about the others but was wisely hiding this behind the excuse of early morning hunting.

"I'll keep the camp-fires burning while you're away," she said when she had tidied herself as best she could in the dark and emerged to find Stephen, a shadowy figure, raking together the embers of the fire.

"You go with me," Stephen said, continuing his ministrations to the fire. "We stay together."

"You know the way well now," Cherry protested. "You couldn't possibly get lost."

"We stay together," Stephen repeated. He looked up but the only light was from the glowing coals and it showed nothing of the expression on his face.

"Don't be tiresome, Cherry," he said. "It's too early in the morning. Can you heat the water and give Peter some powdered milk with it? I'll see how our second duck looks after a night in the coal bed."

Cherry made no reply but gathered some dried leaves and twigs together and heaped them on the coals so that, quickly catching, they threw up bright flames of light. She went back to the rug enclosure and stirred Peter.

If only she had quantities of that lovely clear water with which to wash him! Suddenly she was glad Stephen was insisting that they stay together. Theoretically he was right, of course. She must stop arguing with him, in the long run he was always right.

When the water was warmed and Peter given his drink,

Stephen broke open the clay case of the second duck and they had some of the flesh which was still warm. Peter was given the jellied juice from last night's bird with a biscuit and this time Cherry did not protest. Nothing had happened to the small child during the night as a result of his fatty diet the night before.

Stephen was right once again and Cherry was thankful he didn't labour it.

The fire sprang up brightly enough for them to tidy the camp, dress Peter, gather their small load of waterbags, gun and cartridges, and Peter's shoulder-seat. Cherry made a bundle of her own and Peter's washing. Stephen did likewise with some of his own.

"Please let me carry Peter this morning," Cherry pleaded. "He hasn't quite woken up yet, and with the shoulder bag he's not really any weight."

"Very well, for the first stage at any event. As soon as it's light enough we'll leave. Meantime I'll bank up the fire. We don't want to find ourselves burnt out if and when we get back."

In silence Stephen worked around the camp, burying the scraps of bird bone and washing the utensils in the water from the hole. Cherry tidied Peter and then stole a few minutes to comb her own hair.

Next time she was plane- or ship-wrecked she would remember to bring a brush with her. She wondered if Tracy had another private cache in which there was a hairbrush. How did Tracy keep herself so perfectly groomed?

Cherry had slept in the slacks she had worn the day before so this morning, in view of the fact there was a lake full of washing water only a few miles away, she felt entitled to put on fresh clothes from the case that had been salvaged from the plane.

Her mind went back to that day in the Street of the Pines when she had so suddenly and resolutely made up her mind she would buy slacks.

How pained Mummy had been, but what a wonderful buy they'd turned out to be! Imagine living in this jungle in dresses and skirts!

Thinking of this made Cherry anxious again for the distress her parents would be suffering just now. She went on unthinkingly combing her hair and patting it down with her fingers, as she stood by the fire waiting for Stephen to give the word to move out. What would they be doing now, down there in that little house by the sea?

Stephen had just slung Peter's hammock up among the branches of a tree, against intrusion from ground insects, and turned round, when he caught sight of Cherry, peering into the polished surface of the milk tin lid, and caressing her wayward fringe back into place.

He stood looking at her for a moment. Had Cherry lifted her head she would have seen that faintly amused smile that had annoyed her so much when he had sat in the small living-room of her home down south.

"You should take a leaf out of Tracy's book," he said, walking across the space and picking up the gun. "She carries a little flat brush in her pocket. Always."

"Here we go again," Cherry thought. "Tracy can do no wrong in his eyes."

"I wondered how she did it," she replied, coming out of her thoughtful trance. "Her hair always looks so polished."

She picked up Peter. Stephen, propping the gun against a tree, helped to fit the child into the leg-holes of the shoulder-bag. They were very close and Cherry felt dwarfed beside his tall body and broad shoulders. She looked at him over Peter's head and his eyes met hers.

"Good morning," he said. "I don't believe we mentioned it before."

Cherry smiled. It was going to be peace between them.

"Lovely morning," she said, feeling unexpectedly happy. "Rule number one for the day. I shall stop being jealous of Tracy."

Peter's hat had become awry in these operations and Stephen now straightened it.

"Why doesn't this child ever cry?" Stephen asked.

"Because he's surrounded with love, and happens to be enjoying this strange adventure."

Stephen turned and took the gun again.

"You sound as if you are enjoying it yourself this morning."

"I am," said Cherry. "Look, there's the light coming into the sky. Do we go now?"

"Yes, we'll get a move on now. The sooner your mind's at rest the better, I suppose. You still worrying about Tracy running off with Alan Donnelly?"

Cherry, hugging Peter close to her, endeavoured not to look annoyed.

"I'm worrying about both Tracy and Alan," she said, pressing her lips together. "And in spite of your casual manner, I believe you are worrying, too."

Stephen raised his eyebrows.

"How astute you are. Must be the early morning duck for breakfast. By the way, I thought you didn't like duck?"

The morning was indeed lovely so Cherry didn't allow herself to be cross. The very fact he teased her a little meant their relationship was easier.

CHAPTER TEN

Light came creeping through the trees and the vast tangle of undergrowth like a beautiful wraith. The scents of the bush; of leaves and trees and creepers assailed them with a magic charm.

No, Cherry had to forget her own small vanities. What did it matter that he had never taken much notice of her; that she had been no more than a slightly prissy girl standing the first test of being interviewed for a job; and then passing through the second phase of his acquaintance with her, a mere travelling appendage being taken home to his station to help his sister-in-law bring up her children? What did it matter that on the station she had been a quiet nobody in the kitchen and around the verandas, looking after small Peter when she should have been drilling bigger

Sandra in the skills of reading, writing and arithmetic?

"See yourself as others see you," she had had to say to herself. "Then I was *nobody* but now I'm *somebody* because I'm stranded in the middle of the bush with him. We, we just can't help being something to one another, can we?

"Because he's a man he's got to look after me and Peter. Because I'm a girl I've got to be looked after, and I've got to follow where I'm led. Meantime it's a lovely morning and in no time now I'll have a bath. And so will Peter."

"You seem happy this morning," Stephen remarked.

Cherry smiled up at him.

"Perhaps it's the way you cook duck," she replied.

For a moment he looked surprised, not at her words but at her bright elusive smile.

"Let's go and shoot some more," he said agreeably. "We'll cook it in the coals for lunch too."

He had the gun under his arm and now he picked up the bags in one of which he had already packed such utensils as he thought they might need on their new excursion. He broke through the screen of bushes, held the bushes back with the butt of the gun so that Cherry, carrying Peter, could pass through, and five minutes later they were well on their way down the trail that led to the lake.

They had covered half the distance when Stephen called a halt under the ancient cabbage tree beyond which Cherry had not been able to find the trail yesterday.

"Five minutes' rest, and change burdens," said Stephen.

Peter had been kicking and wriggling for the last ten minutes. Cherry felt that he at least needed a change so she gladly agreed.

Stephen had to help free Peter's chubby legs from the carrying-bag before she could set him on the ground. Again she had that pleasant feeling of them both, herself and Stephen, being in closer companionship. The going had been hard and as they had had to go in single file they had hardly spoken since they left the camp.

Peter, on the ground, hooted with delight at this new environment. He immediately began to scrabble around where he was sitting for new wonders with which to play; a broken stick and several tree nuts.

"Sit down and rest," said Stephen.

Cherry did so, leaning her back against the tree-trunk and drawing her knees up under her. Stephen did likewise and they were shoulder to shoulder. The tree-trunk though large was rounded.

Stephen searched a moment in his pockets, then frowning, let his hands fall. Cherry knew what had happened. From habit he had been looking for a cigarette and then remembered they were forbidden until shared.

Cherry with a smile of triumph produced a packet of cigarettes from her pocket. She drew a cigarette from the packet and handed it delicately to Stephen between her thumb and forefinger; the rest of her hand and arm had the stylised gesture of a ballet dancer. Mischievously Cherry was telling him in pantomime that here was a packet from Tracy's cache.

Stephen frowned, then relaxed and smiled.

"Where did you find them?" he said. He still did not take the cigarette.

"Growing in the bushes behind our private camp. You know, the way Moses grew in the rushes. And there's plenty more."

Stephen was only of half a mind to take the cigarette but Cherry leaned forward and held it close to his nose.

"You needn't smoke it," she said. "Just smell it."

Stephen smiled, took the cigarette and put it in his mouth. Then began the futile search for matches in his pockets.

Cherry bided her time, and then took out a box from the same pocket whence came the cigarettes. She struck a match and held it to the tip of his cigarette. When he had drawn deeply, she flicked out the match and put the box back in her pocket. She wrapped her arms round her legs and gazed innocently in front of her. Stephen shook away the first ash and regarded Cherry's profile with curiosity.

"Do you know," he said at length, "if I had a wife

I'd rather she found me a cigarette in a moment of dire need than be able to roast duck for dinner."

"What a wonderful wife I'll make someone," said Cherry. "I find cigarettes growing on bushes and I can't roast duck in a coal-fire."

"That's something worth remembering," said Stephen lazily. Then he looked at Cherry through smoke-hazed eyes. "I must tell Alan. He's looking for a wife. But what happens to the man down south?"

"What man down south?" asked Cherry, surprised.

"The one you promised to return to . . . one year to the day, I think you said."

"Oh!" said Cherry, suddenly deflated.

She was lolling here having fun and all the time, somewhere down there a thousand miles away, her father and mother were sitting, their ears glued to the radio, the papers shaking in their hands.

Here she was, momentarily happy, and down there in the Street of the Pines Dad and Mum were being made sick with anxiety.

"Stephen," she said, "how soon can we get out of here? You said you found where the jungle ends and the plains begin. How long before we can make the plains? Will searching aircraft see us there?"

"What do you think I'm carrying in this bag? Why do you think I made Tracy and Alan take waterbags yesterday? When we've collected as many birds and as much water as we can carry between us, we'll head for the plains to-day."

"Oh," said Cherry, relieved. "Thank goodness. They must be worrying about us back home——"

"Of course. And now to take your mind off their troubles just look at that new one growing up over there."

Cherry followed Stephen's eyes to where Peter was no longer sitting on the ground. He was elevated on all fours, his knees and elbows stiff, holding himself balanced in a position that he wasn't quite certain he could control.

Stephen drew in his legs as if to rise, but Cherry put out her hand and stopped him.

"Don't, don't!" she pleaded urgently. "He's going to stand up."

"How do you know?"

"I don't know. I think. I've never seen a baby stand up for the first time. But I think . . ."

"The maternal instinct, eh? There really is such a thing."

"Ssh!" said Cherry. "Don't move." Her hand rested on Stephen's arm, holding it firmly so that he would not stand up and interrupt the child in the performance of this first adult rite.

It seemed an age that Peter remained in that curious four-legged position.

"Oh!" said Cherry, in agony. "If only he'd put his feet a little closer together, he'd make it."

Peter's hands lifted an inch from the ground. He wavered, then slowly, with concentrated patience he straightened his back. Suddenly he was seeing the world from a new angle. There was a look of sheer astonishment on his face. His eyes were wide with wonder.

He looked at Cherry and Stephen, and, wordless, they looked back at him. Then slowly over Peter's face there spread an expression of satisfied, seraphic joy. He knew he'd done a wonderful thing. One foot came forward in a first step then he lost balance and sat down on his seat with a plonk.

"O-oh!" said Cherry and slowly expelled a breath of joy herself! She was quite unconscious of the fact she held Stephen's arm and that her eyes were wet.

Stephen looked at his self-satisfied nephew, then at Cherry's face. He pulled in the corners of his mouth and scratched the back of his neck with his left hand.

"I'm a grown man and have been walking for thirty years," he said. "And I haven't seen anyone shed tears over that fact yet."

"I'm not crying," said Cherry, thrusting away the arm which she had held so tightly, and brushing her hand across her eyes. "I'm smiling."

She jumped up and ran across the clearing to the child. She knelt down in front of him and took his hands.

"Come on, Peter," she said, cajoling. "Do it again, darling."

Stephen unlooped himself from his sitting position under the tree, picked up the carrying-bag and went towards her.

"You're a strange person if ever there was one," he said, addressing the top of Cherry's head. "One minute you're worrying as to whether Tracy is man-eating Alan Donnelly, at the same time trying to hustle the whole party out on the plains to send lovelorn messages down south. Next moment you're prepared to waste hours of time watching a small boy learning to walk."

"You're heartless," said Cherry, standing up and picking Peter up in her arms. She gave the child a warm hug and then helped settle him in the carrying-bag which Stephen already had over his shoulder. She looked at Stephen again. "And I don't think you're very kind about Alan Donnelly."

"And I think you're too kind. He's a grown man and can fend for himself, you know."

"Of course I know. I'm only particularly nice to him because it was his plane that landed us in this mess. He must feel responsible, though he doesn't say anything."

"He didn't land us in this mess. A bolt of lightning did. And the insurance will pay for the plane," he said abruptly, then added, "I'll take the gun, you take the bag, Cherry."

"Peter's heavy and he wriggles. I'll take the gun and both bags."

"You will not," said Stephen. "I never trust a woman with a gun."

"Thank you," said Cherry tartly. "I don't like guns anyway."

"Right," said Stephen. "That settles that argument equably. Well, are you ready? Then on our way."

Oddly enough it had been a pleasant interlude, that short rest under the cabbage tree. The tendency to argue between herself and Stephen could hardly be called real argument, Cherry thought. It had been more like friendly badinage. It was rather nice like this. Sort of friendly. She felt she had come a long way to seeing a nicer side of Stephen's character. In fact, getting to know him.

And as for young Peter taking his first step in the middle of a jungle! Well, really, the early morning was full of mysterious wonders!

Cherry thrust her way through bushes happily as she followed Stephen and the baby.

"It's lovely," she thought. "Really lovely. If only we could go on for ever. For ever and ever, with short stops for a nice clean bath, of course." Momentarily she had forgotten the rest of the world.

Stephen had his own thought processes as his eyes, without direction from conscious thought, picked out the marks that showed the way.

She was a quaint little thing, was Cherry Landin.

His mind went back to the picture of the young girl running across the white sands of the Indian Ocean in her blue swimsuit, the sun shining on her hair, as youth and the sheer physical joy of living shone like an aura from her whole physical being.

He had been amused at her sweet youth, at her girlish anxiety to get into the water lest the water would not wait for her.

Then she had turned out to be the prospective governess for his brother's children.

"Well, well," he had thought. "Wonders will never cease. So inexperienced and willing to go away for a whole year from that over-cloistered and cosseted hearth of the Landins." He had wondered, rather briefly, how anyone as inexperienced could possibly manage the two children on Yulinga Station.

And here she was managing Peter, the younger and tougher, from Stephen's point of view, of the two children as if Peter was her own, and she'd been managing babies all her short life.

Stephen, holding his nephew close to him as he thrust his way between trees, and through and over heavy undergrowth, smiled to himself.

He rather liked the way Tracy fooled the world. Much

more worldly, of course, than the girl ploughing her way through the jungle behind him. Yet oddly enough Cherry was attractive in her quaint quasi-old-world way, and, as Alan Donnelly had remarked, as game as Ned Kelly. Alan had something of a reputation of being a man for the ladies. Stephen hoped Cherry wouldn't get hurt. He was no longer smiling, but frowning now as he pursued this train of thought.

He emerged from the tree fringe to find Tracy and Alan Donnelly camped a hundred yards away from where he now stood with Peter in his arms. There was a fire burning and Tracy was busy cooking something on the end of a long forked stick.

Alan let out a whoop of delight and came towards Stephen. Tracy, more leisurely, put down her bush fork, pushed her hair back into place and began to pick her way delicately over the stones and broken tree debris on the high bank above the lake.

"Well, you're a fine pair," said Stephen. "Took too long swimming, I suppose?"

Alan grinned.

"Ask Tracy," he said. He looked inquiringly first at Stephen then into the dark tunnels of the bush. "Where's Cherry?"

"Following along," said Stephen, looking back over his shoulder, expecting to see Cherry appearing between the trees.

There was a momentary silence between the two men and in that moment it was quite obvious there was a silence in the bush too. There was no sound of anyone approaching.

The grin disappeared from Alan Donnelly's face. His voice was suddenly sharp.

"Where's Cherry?" he said. "Damn it, man, where is she? You haven't left her behind? In there? In that damn' jungle?"

He thrust past Stephen and pushed into the bush.

"Cherry!" he shouted. "Cherry! Cherry!"

Stephen's face had frozen.

"Tracy," he said quietly. "Come here and get Peter."

It took several minutes to free Peter from the shoulder bag and settle him safely in Tracy's arms.

"Don't be long, for goodness' sake," Tracy said. "I'll never manage this wriggling elephant for more than five minutes for sure."

Stephen did not answer. He turned and thrust back into the bush. Twenty yards back along the trail he stopped and listened. He could hear Alan Donnelly thundering on and over and through the undergrowth with the noise of half a dozen elephants as he did it. Beyond that noise he heard Cherry's clear voice.

"Here! This way, Alan. I'm all right."

Alan in his ardour to get there would never follow the sound of her voice, Stephen thought. And if Cherry was unhurt and just being difficult he would tell her with considerable forcefulness that there were certain pranks *not* played when, fun and all though the adventure might be, their lives actually were in jeopardy.

Stephen strode on through the bush in anger.

Tracy was the only one other than himself who knew the real dangers of that jungle. Poisoned bushes, small snakes and even pythons, were negligible beside the horrors of getting lost in it. He had carefully kept this knowledge from Alan and Cherry. On himself he had taken the responsibility of watching their every footstep, of eating before they did, of testing leaves, sticks and bush fronds before Peter had been allowed to be put down amongst them. And a burden that responsibility had been.

Cherry had adopted proprietorial rights over Peter and good and all though this might be in its appropriate place, in an insect and snake infested jungle this was a responsibility she was not equipped to undertake. All very well on a homestead veranda, or a comfortable seat in a plane.

Alan Donnelly, having had a start on Stephen, got to Cherry first.

She was sitting on the ground, in a nest of bushes and smiling.

"Don't look so worried," she said brightly. "It's only my foot. I caught it in the creepers, and tripped. I think my ankle's swelling a bit."

Alan was beside her in a minute and sank down on one knee. Their two heads nearly touched as they bent to look at the ankle. They looked up simultaneously and their eyes met. Alan wiped the sweat from his forehead with the back of his hand.

"You gave me an awful fright, Cherry," he said. "I thought you were lost. Why didn't you call out to Stephen?"

"I heard your voices. I wanted him to get through to the lake and put Peter down first. He couldn't help me with Peter in his arms. Besides, I thought if I rested a minute I'd get up and hobble after him. Anyhow——"

"Anyhow what?"

"You got lost yourself, last night," she said reproachfully. "I worried too."

"I wish I had that honest excuse," he said ruefully. "I'm afraid it was no more than that Tracy liked swimming so much I couldn't persuade her out of the water before the sun began to go down behind the trees."

"Were you *swimming* with her?" demanded Cherry primly.

"No such luck. A hundred yards away," grinned Alan. "That's why I couldn't get her out of the water."

They looked at one another and laughed.

They were thus, Alan on one knee before Cherry and Cherry, one slightly swollen ankle thrust out before her, sitting back on her two hands, her head thrown back and laughing, when Stephen burst through the bushes.

He stopped and took stock of the scene.

Alan failed to see the irritation in his face.

"She's all right, old man," Alan said. "Not lost, merely injured."

Stephen walked over to the couple, and standing stiffly looked down at Cherry's foot.

"Not very bad," he said dryly. "Why didn't you call out?"

Cherry sensed at once the anger behind Stephen's expressionless face.

"There wasn't any need," she said. "I would have come on in a minute or two. I was safe here and I could hear voices——"

"Next time think of other people as well as yourself," Stephen said. "I'm sorry to have to exercise my authority like this, Cherry, but I've told you – we stay together. No one member of the party shall be *anywhere* – I repeat – *anywhere* out of sight of another."

Cherry began to scramble up and Alan helped her.

"She's safe and sound, that's the main thing," said Alan by way of making peace.

"Is Peter all right?" Cherry asked Stephen. She had no answer to his recrimination.

"He's with Tracy," Stephen said dryly. He added, "She knows a good deal more about the nature of this country and the right places to put a child, or a grown woman for that matter, in the undergrowth."

"What was wrong with the bush I was sitting on?" asked Cherry. "It was a nice soft one."

Stephen looked at her as if he would like to smack her first and explain afterwards. He did neither.

"There are bushes, and bushes," he said cryptically. "Let's leave it at that."

Cherry took a step on her injured foot.

"Ouch!" she said, then tied her mouth up in knots so that she wouldn't say that again.

Stephen stopped and looked at her, then over his shoulder at Alan.

"I'd better carry her," he said. He was taller and his shoulders were much broader than Alan's.

"I'm all right," protested Cherry.

"We'll decide that when we get out of here." He bent down and swung her up in his arms. In an effortless way he began to weave his way amongst the trees and through the undergrowth.

Cherry felt guilty, also sorry that the pleasant companionship of the early morning had disappeared and that in its place there was one large angry man and a slightly injured and foolish girl.

"It's quite nice up here," she said brightly. "Now I know why Peter likes you carrying him. It's high up."

"Just keep quiet and let's get out of here," said Stephen tersely.

"It was nice of you to carry me, Stephen," said Cherry, "but now I know why I thought my bushes were soft. Things are a bit prickly round this part of the world right now."

Stephen had stooped and twisted a little to dodge a tree on one side and get under another on the other side. His head bent down and their faces touched. Cherry smiled and for a moment she thought she saw its reflection in his own grey eyes.

"I won't do it again," she promised. "Besides it hurts."

They had reached the edge of the lake and he set her down so that she stood upright on both her feet. She steadied herself on his arm.

"That's all right," he said in a softer note. "We'd better look at that foot. If we want to make the plains to-day we've a long walk ahead."

"And you can't carry me *all* the way," said Cherry brightly, and smoothing down her clothes with both her hands. Over Stephen's shoulder she caught sight of Tracy. "My goodness, where's Peter?"

"Crawling about somewhere," said Tracy.

Stephen spun round and Cherry started forward, hesitated as her injured foot made itself felt, then stopped dead. Twenty-five yards away Peter was standing up beside a small bush. He gave a yelp of delight, took first one step, then another, then fell back into a sitting position. He looked astonished for a minute, then seeing that the world was safe and right way up he beamed.

Cherry, staring at him, was still holding Stephen's arm, partly to balance herself and partly because she had forgotten she was even touching him.

"Call that crawling?" she said with scorn to Tracy, "The man is *walking*——"

"Oh," said Tracy. "A pity you don't take a leaf out of his book."

Cherry dropped Stephen's arm as if it had been a hot rail she had been holding.

"Why!" she thought, "Tracy minds my holding Stephen's arm. But of course . . . I'd forgotten, there's some sort of understanding between them. How crazy can a girl get!" She pushed her fingers through her hair as if to brush cobwebs out of her mind. "I'd actually forgotten."

She started to walk forward across the stony surface of the ground towards the child. She gritted her teeth hard against showing any expression of pain.

Her ankle hurt badly but Stephen had said they had quite a walk to the plains and it was unthinkable that she, Cherry, should hold them up.

"Uh-huh," said Tracy to Stephen. She stood with her arms akimbo, one foot arched and pointed, tapping the ground lightly. "And just exactly why did you have to carry her, Stephen? I've a theory our little governess was putting on an act."

Cherry had reached Peter and she knelt down beside him, taking his two hands in her own and trying to encourage him, to try that momentous business of standing up and walking again. She had her back to the others.

Stephen pulled his ear irritably.

"Her ankle is swollen," he said. "I should have left the ministrations to Alan."

"Of course. The histrionics were intended for him, didn't you know? She really has got something, has our Cherry. Not so dull-witted after all."

Stephen looked at Tracy.

"You kept Alan camped out all night, a whole jungle away. Nobody was very pleased about that, you know."

Tracy looked at him with lazy eyes and beautifully arched brows. She smiled serenely.

"So long as you noticed my absence, darling."

"I did. And Cherry noticed Alan's absence."

"Then what's wrong with a perfect morning? Come on, we've got fish for breakfast."

When Cherry presently rose, with Peter in her arms, and

came somewhat haltingly towards the fire, she saw Stephen turn abruptly away.

The friendly guide through the jungle had gone, and the distant stranger was back.

"The sooner we've had some refreshment the sooner we can move on," he said to Tracy.

Cherry felt he intended her to know he was not going to allow her injured ankle to hold them up: and for the moment he had nothing more to say to her.

Cherry's heart dropped a little.

It was seeing Tracy and Alan so comfortably camped down here that had changed Stephen's mood so quickly, she surmised. Her own ankle wasn't as bad as all that.

CHAPTER ELEVEN

Alan Donnelly had come out of the jungle and gone straight to the fire. He was now turning fish over on hot flat stones.

Cherry came closer to the cooking scene and sat down on a rock, holding the child. Her foot hurt a little. She must hide the fact by pretending she had to sit down to hold the small child. Peter was wholly concerned with what was going on round the fire. Temporarily he had forgotten the new world he had discovered by being able to stand upright. Here was another, and quite different, to engage his interest.

"How did you catch fish?" asked Cherry with wonder.

Alan straightened himself up. He pointed his long pronged stick first at Stephen and then Tracy.

"They might know all about bush-whacking," he said. "But it takes an air pilot to know about fishing when you haven't got a line."

He looked slightly smug but Cherry felt happy for his sake that he had achieved something to impress the others.

"How did you do it? Trap them?" asked Stephen.

"More or less," said Alan, back to the business of turning fish. "I go crayfishing off the west coast in my holidays.

I used the cray-pot idea. Make a pot of stones with a hole for entry at the top. Put the innards of the water-hen we cooked for dinner last night in the sea-pot and anchored them down with small stones."

He looked over his shoulder and grinned boyishly at Cherry.

"Sheep are silly," he said, "but nothing like as silly as fish. In through the top hole they go to get a cheap feed and forget to find their way out again. This not-so-silly human got up at daybreak, dropped in a hefty stone and temporarily stunned them; lifted them out, five of the beauties – *voilà*, grilled breakfast for the family."

"Very clever!" Cherry said appreciatively. She wanted to be pleasant to make up for the momentary touch of ill-will she had sensed in Tracy when Stephen had carried her through the bush. "You two seem to have got yourself a good time last night. Roast water-hen for dinner and fish-potting for breakfast."

"Don't be jealous, darling," said Tracy. "He slept one side of that pile of rocks and I slept the other. We didn't even need Peter for a chaperon."

Cherry flushed. She wasn't used to such frank talk and she certainly was too unsophisticated to have the kind of thoughts that flitted through Tracy's mind.

Both Tracy and Stephen seemed to be amused that she was the kind of person who needed chaperons, just for the look of the thing. Hadn't he teased her about it last night?

As Stephen had said, lost persons couldn't be choosers but all the same there wasn't anything unwholesome in those old-world fashions.

Obliquely Cherry felt she was in defence of her parents and their way of life again. She had seen Tracy cast a derisive smile at Stephen as if she was sharing some kind of joke with him. Cherry wondered if at some time, since her arrival at Yulinga, Stephen had told the others about her formal and "quaint" little mother.

She bit her lip.

"Safe to give Peter fish do you think, Alan?" she asked.

"Nothing safer and nothing better," he replied as if

Tracy's little by-play had gone over his head, or wasn't worth his notice.

Stephen had crouched down on his heels to watch Alan's cooking prowess. Tracy handed him a cigarette out of her packet and so engrossed was he in the business of grilling fish on hot stones that he accepted the cigarette, took a stick from the fire and applied the coal end to his smoke, without realising what he did. He had not noticed that, once again, Tracy had produced something that was supposed to be communal property and in Stephen's keeping, not her own.

He got up now and reached for his gun.

"Keep mine hot while I do a spot of shooting," he said. "I don't want all the duck to leave before I've bagged enough for a couple of days."

Cherry looked over the lake. There were plenty of brown duck about but the coveys of pelicans and other birds had gone. It was mid-morning now and she supposed they had taken off soon after daybreak.

"Bathe first or eat first?" Alan said, standing up and looking at Cherry.

"Will the fish spoil if we bathe? I mean me and Peter?"

"Not if you're quick."

"We'll be quick," said Cherry.

She stood up and once again her foot hurt. She winced unthinkingly.

Alan came across to her.

"I'll carry Peter," he said.

"Thank you." She gave up the load willingly.

"And would you like a loan of my arm?"

"Yes, please," said Cherry, "but not while Stephen and Tracy are looking."

They stood and waited until the other pair had begun their descent down the uneven slope of the bank to the lake's edge.

"Now," said Alan conspiratorially, "we'll go this way. I'll help you bath Peter and then bring him back while you swim. Leave the washing until after we've eaten."

"Good," said Cherry. "And, Alan, when you come back there's an empty tin for a billy, the plastic cups and the packet of tea from the pilot's ration box in the bigger of the two bags we brought. Do you think we could . . ." She smiled up at him. "Do you think we might just have some tea as a special treat?"

"Since that pair are smoking illicit cigarettes, I think we might do a spot of wrongdoing ourselves," Alan said with a grin. "Hurry back, Cherry. There'll be tea for two before they've had time to bring down a brace of ducklings."

"And I've got secrets in my pocket," said Cherry, patting the place where she had some of Tracy's cigarettes hidden. "I just might take to smoking myself to prove my independence."

They were picking their way carefully round the stony outcrops and downwards towards the place where Cherry had had her swim yesterday. Alan had Peter on one arm and Cherry holding firmly to the other.

"Dear girl, don't take to smoking," pleaded Alan. "I can do enough of that for the two of us."

Cherry stopped, dropped his arm and fished for the cigarettes. She took out one, gave it to him and then handed him the matches.

Alan struck a match, drew in the cigarette smoke happily and then expelled it slowly.

"What on earth do hermits do without women?" he asked. "No one to think up crime for them."

Twenty minutes later, beautifully refreshed, Cherry climbed up the bank and joined the others already sitting down for their fish meal.

Stephen, with Tracy as retriever, had been quicker at bringing down duck than Cherry had anticipated. Tracy, prettily wet – she was never anything but pretty, wet or dry – was already steaming out in the hot sun. Cherry's hair was almost dry by the time she climbed up the short bank of the lake. Peter, tired now with his early morning activities, was asleep on Alan's shirt under a tree near the bush edge.

"I gave him a drink of tea," Alan explained triumphantly when Cherry arrived. "After all, he can walk. He's a grown man now."

Stephen frowned.

"Good for you," said Cherry. "Tea is quite harmless when given in small doses. I trust it was weak, Alan?"

"Strong as a blackfellow likes it," said Alan. "Look at the tan he's got on him. How do you expect to make a giant of him if you feed him on wish-wash?"

All this was badinage which both Alan and Cherry were enjoying. Cherry knew that Alan had set himself to be helpful and that he would give Peter nothing that would harm him. Stephen was frowning because he didn't know whence had come the tea in the first place and in the second place this dickering with Peter's diet was playing with the fortunes of his nephew. He regarded himself as responsible for what happened to young Peter.

Tracy, meantime, delicately ate fish flesh with her fingers, all the time making pretty gestures with her hands that never let anyone forget she was a dancer.

"Whose child are you talking about?" she said, licking the tips of her two fingers as tenderly and elegantly as if this was something only the best ballerinas do on the stage of Covent Garden.

"Ours," said Cherry and Alan in unison.

They caught one another's eyes, and laughed.

"Hurry up and have your joint breakfast," said Stephen shortly. "We're moving out of here in just half an hour. We want to make camp on the plains by sundown. That is if your injuries permit, Cherry."

"They permit," said Cherry. She had sat down to take her fish which Alan was now serving to her on a flat small stone. She drew her injured foot under her so that no one would notice that it was now black and blue around the ankle bone.

They reached the plains at least an hour before sundown and this was due more to good fortune than Cherry's stoicism. Each quarter of a mile Stephen had gone on ahead to make sure of the way. Quite by accident he had come on a section of the bush that had thinned out to scrub and low stunted trees. Through this area he had been able to see distant low hills that were not tree-covered at all. He estimated that they had broken through to the plain about three miles north of the path he had discovered the morning before.

Cherry, determined not to hold up the party, had for once willingly surrendered Peter to Alan Donnelly's care. Stephen was fully taken up with the problems of path finding; carrying the gun and the birds he had killed that morning. Tracy and Cherry shared the bag load of a change of clothes and the utensils which, fortunately being plastic, were very light. In addition there were two of the waterbags and the bag of emergency food and dried milk for Peter. Alan carried the largest of the waterbags as well as Peter.

On Stephen's command they had eaten well at the lakeside camp and they drank as much water as they could comfortably take. This meant if there was no anxiety about food and water they could take longer reconnoitring the conditions for a long camp on the plains. Clearly if there was no available water they would have to return to the lake.

Already it was taken for granted they had permanently left the camp in the clearing near the wrecked plane.

"We're within a few miles of the lake and water and food," Stephen had said when they reached the plain. "We can make camp here and return there if necessary. In no time now we should be spotted from the air."

With his usual thoroughness and vigilance he set about making a camp at sufficient distance from the scrub to ensure safety from setting it on fire. Here, away from the deep heavy cool growth of the jungle, the bush was dry as tinder.

It was strange, Cherry thought, that within so short a distance of one another there should be both near-desert and dense growth. It was as if the monsoonal rains that watered the north stopped dead on the same latitude every year. The poor sparse plain before them, the rounded treeless hills in the distance looked as if they had never seen rain. The heat was drier but very fierce.

Oh, now, for that lovely lake bath they had left five hours earlier!

"I don't trust scrub. You girls will have to sleep out in

the open the same as we do," Stephen ordered. " I'll make two camp-fires. Tracy, you and Cherry sleep Peter between you, as usual."

" I'll give him to Cherry for the night," said Tracy. " He hasn't got a cot any more, and I don't like being kicked."

" Perhaps Cherry might feel the same way," Stephen said quietly. His voice sounded judicial and not angry. He was doing the right thing by all members of the party.

" I don't mind a bit," Cherry said hastily.

" And she's paid for it," said Tracy.

" Quite right," said Cherry unexpectedly. " I am paid by Mr. and Mrs. Denton to take charge of Peter. He's mine until I stop getting paid. Now please . . . no one interfere."

This she meant for Stephen who showed every now and again a propensity for interfering on the grounds that he was the child's uncle.

" Left alone," Cherry thought, " she would do far more good for Peter than all the combined interferences of relatives and friends.

" Heavens, how was she ever going to give him up when this trip was over?"

Cherry was sitting down on a fallen tree-trunk just beyond the verge of the bush, giving Peter a further drink of pow-dered milk and one of the few remaining biscuits.

" They'll find us any minute now, sweetie-pie," she said to the small boy. " So I won't be counting the biscuits so often."

She was suddenly aware that the noise of activity on the part of the other three had stopped. There was an odd silence all around. She looked up.

All three were standing, their hands shading their eyes and looking to the west. They had seen something of interest and yet not one of them had spoken.

" What is it?" asked Cherry. She had Peter on one arm and the plastic cup that held his milk in the other hand so she could not shade her eyes against the westering sun. To the west, where they were looking with such con-centration, there was nothing but a plain of dried grasses and a glaring sky beyond the rounded hummock of low hills.

The three continued to stand in silence, looking.

At last Stephen dropped his hand and turned to Tracy. " Did you see what I saw?" he said.

Tracy nodded. She smiled. Stephen lifted his shoulders in a quick gesture and Tracy did a small hurray in panto-mime. She waved one hand in a circle round her head and then struck a pose that seemed to say . . . " What do you think of that?"

Cherry knew that the two of them, Stephen and Tracy, were at that moment not only cut off from Alan and herself by virtue of their background and relatives but they were cut off by their bush know-how too.

Alan was seeing something but he was as ignorant of what he was seeing, as Tracy and Stephen were conversant.

Cherry felt a little stab of anger.

Whatever it was they were looking at it meant something important in the lives of five stranded people, and they hadn't the kindness to explain it.

No, thought Cherry. She wouldn't like to be married to a man like Stephen. He was clannish, and he was superior. He didn't care about ordinary people like herself and Alan. It was absurd for him to think that Tracy was any use to him, even if she did know bushcraft, while she herself and Alan had carried on with the chores unremittingly.

" We are servants. We are of no real importance. Alan is the salaried officer of an airline which is paid to convey the Dentons of the world backwards and forwards between their town houses and their station properties. And I'm the paid governess!"

She felt angry, for, irrespective of their various positions in life, at this moment in time they were all in the same spot. They had been plane-wrecked and were lost. Somewhere out there Stephen and Tracy were looking at salvation and they didn't even bother to tell Alan and herself about it.

Cherry's foot hurt her, and she was hot and tired.

She felt suddenly ashamed.

" I think they see something," she said, drawing Peter

closer. " I think they see something wonderful, and in a minute they'll tell us."

At that moment Alan Donnelly spoke.

"Well, what is it?" he said to Stephen. "It's not a willy-willy. It's static."

"It's cattle moving in a mob. It couldn't be anything else. A dust cloud as big as that means a native corroboree or cattle on the move. It's the wrong hour of the day for corroboree, so it's cattle."

Tracy struck another pose and waved her slender hand in the air.

"And if you look at those streaks in the bright blue heavens you'll see another reason why they're cattle."

"Good heavens," said Alan Donnelly. "More birds and not flying inland to that lake."

"No," said Stephen. "They're flying in to a water-hole. And it's at water-holes that drovers camp down their mobs for the night."

He turned round. Suddenly his whole face was changed. It was creased with that illuminating smile Cherry had seen on the day he had come to the home in the Street of the Pines.

"Good people," he said, "we are somewhere very near a stock route. Sometime to-day that mob may have passed this way. I've been worried by a dust haze ever since we broke through into the scrub from the heavy bush."

Cherry, looking at his face as he spoke, felt unexpectedly moved. She was remorseful for her unkind thoughts of a moment ago.

Except for their short interlude alone this morning Stephen had not been very friendly or companionable with any of them. Now for the first time she understood he had had a burden of worry on his shoulders which somewhere in a sternly disciplined mind he had hidden from them all.

His had truly been the authority and the leadership. This extraordinary change in his face which made him look younger now proved it.

Somewhere not many miles away was a saviour in the form of a cattle drover.

"Well," said Stephen, still smiling, "I think that speaks two roast ducks for dinner, two biscuits for Peter and a cigarette all round."

He dug his hands in his belt, rocked back on his heels and lifted his face to the sky.

"Even the craziest aeroplane can find a mob of cattle," he said.

Alan gaily threw more wood on the fire which they had already got going.

"Steady on your abuse of aircraft," he said with a grin. "Next time I wreck you I'll put the sea between you and any mob of cattle."

"Yes," thought Cherry with compunction, "he does feel that aeroplane crash. He's making a joke of it but he knows that his own personal troubles are only just beginning."

"Alan," she said, "thank you for crash landing us the way you did. It was wonderful. Any other pilot would have made a mess of it."

"Oh, and thank Stephen and me for guiding you to safety through python-writhing jungles, waterless wastes of scrub and poison-infested bush," said Tracy.

She too threw a piece of wood on the fire. In a minute all three of them were stooping, gathering small broken sticks and twig ends and throwing them on the fire. They were like children playing at snowballs in a different land and climate.

"I wish I'd seen a python," said Cherry, not believing in them and also wanting to say something funny and brave and carefree.

"We ought to have brought home those two we found hanging in the trees yesterday, Stephen darling," Tracy said lightly. "That would have pleased Cherry's idea of seeing life."

"Not really?" said Cherry incredulously. She suddenly hugged Peter closer.

"Yes, really," said Tracy. "Ask Stephen. He all but leaned against one to have a rest on our way home from the lake."

Cherry closed her eyes and when she opened them looked straight across the intervening space at Stephen.

"And you said nothing?" she said.

Stephen's little amused smile did not, for once, annoy her.

"Oh, you wouldn't have understood about pythons," said Tracy airily, taking a dancing step to throw more wood on the fire. "They're quite the thing up here in this part of the world."

Cherry met Alan Donnelly's eyes and they both seemed to say the same thing to one another.

Cherry swallowed.

"Thank you for saying nothing," she said. "I would have been terrified coming through the jungle to-day."

She looked from Stephen to Tracy and back to Stephen again.

Suddenly they both looked different to her. They were both clothed in the secret atmosphere of their nonchalance and their silent bravery. Two people who dealt in pythons! One never had a hair out of place and the other behaved like a slightly irritable man whose main preoccupation was to see the governess did not underfeed his one and only nephew.

"Thanks a lot, old man," Alan said to Stephen across the now blazing fire. "I'll admit I was a bit hipped you would make those path-finding forages on your own. Now I can see your point."

"Tracy was with me," said Stephen. "She'd charm any snake off a tree."

"Out of a basket," said Tracy carelessly. "I've always longed to meet an Indian snake charmer. All I need is a reed pipe."

"Miss Tracy," said Alan, bowing, "I defer to a very grand little lady."

Oddly enough, Cherry felt a pang of jealousy. Ah, if only she could do something grand and heroic!

She looked down at the face of the small child in her lap. He had turned his head and was looking up at her. He smiled with delight as her face turned to his.

"You'll do me," that smile seemed to say. Somehow Cherry felt solaced.

The excitement over, Stephen regained his manner of camp chief and detailed off the immediate chores to the others.

"Tracy," he said, "take charge of that child for a change. Cherry, you had a lesson in cooking last night, you make the earth paste for the ducks and put them under the coals. Never mind the feathers, they'll come off with the case. Alan, you deploy north and see if you can find the cattle tracks that way. Don't lose sight of the camp. Return immediately you begin to lose it. I'm going out on the plain. I might be some time."

"Don't go too far yourself, and get lost," said Cherry, suddenly feeling she couldn't bear to let Stephen out of her sight. He wasn't just man any more, he was of the stuff that gods were made. He had minded them carefully – he had brought them to safety, he had ignored pythons as mere trifles of interest in a day's march.

"It will be time to worry if I'm not back by starlight," he said. "I'm a bushman. I won't get lost."

"That's one for me," said Alan. "I've got to stay in sight of the camp." Then he laughed. "And the ladies too," he added with something that was nearly a wink.

"You'd better," said Stephen grimly. "I've enough on my hands finding cattle tracks without finding lost pilots too."

It occurred to Cherry that Stephen was too tough to be sensitive. He would never know how that occasional tilt at Alan's vocation had an unintended barb in it. Or was it that he was not amused at Alan's jest about remaining in sight of the ladies?

CHAPTER TWELVE

It was indeed starlight before Stephen returned from his foraging out on the plain.

"No luck," he said. "How was it with you, Alan?"

"The same. Not a sign of tracks."

"We'll have to wait till sun-up. They'll be on the move then. We'll get their direction from their dust cloud."

By the firelight of the camp and with the aid of the torch they had examined Alan's maps which he had brought from the plane and which were now useful. The edge of the jungle country and the proximity of the stock route gave them a near location.

"My guess is, it's the Timor Bay stock route," said Stephen. "They're travelling north in a line parallel with the border about three miles across from us. We'll strike camp before daylight and be ready to move as soon as we see their dust cloud."

"You're not anxious about leaving the vicinity of water?" asked Alan.

"No. We're as near that water-hole as we are the lake and we'll conserve what we've got. Meantime we'll make some firebrands of dried sticks in case a plane goes over in the night. If one is heard all hands out and wave the lighted brands."

The cooked ducks had been a success and everyone settled down happily for the night. Their hard travelling might not yet be over and the discomforts would probably continue, yet everyone felt reassured that ultimately they would be found and that now there was an immediate chance of their whereabouts becoming known. This, everyone felt, was of greater importance than their own comfort. Distraught relatives elsewhere were real anxieties to them all.

No plane was heard in the night and by daybreak they were all up and breakfasted on the remains of duck cooked the night before. Peter had his powdered milk and biscuit in addition to his portion of meat juice. This time Cherry made no objections to this diet. Nothing had happened to Peter. He was as well and happy as the days were long and arduous.

Clearly, the primitive way of life was heaven for a child, Cherry thought.

She took Tracy's lack of attention to her sister's child for granted. Tracy had other qualities. And probably didn't like children, anyway. It was a good thing for Peter that Mrs. Denton had indeed sent Cherry along to accompany him on that trip to Timor Bay.

Cherry wondered now if they would ever see Timor Bay. The urgency for Peter's injections had dwindled to a small matter of the future.

They moved out in single file across the plain, Stephen going well ahead. He could map out the land, and would possibly get to the water-hole ahead of them. He could then return with water if the followers were too slow.

Cherry actually was slow because of her injured ankle but she said nothing of this, walking as fast as she could in the heat and tried sorely by a lot of sharp pain.

She thought that everyone else in the party had shown bravery and coolness in one form or another since that lightning had struck the plane and it humiliated her to think she might hold them all up by a petty injury.

She said nothing, hid her limp, took her turn with Alan in carrying Peter or the bags and tried not to be too slow.

It was early afternoon before they crossed the low stony outcrop of hills, sprouting here and there high grass and small dried-up looking prickly bushes. Below them was the lily-strewn water-hole and all the evidences of a major camp from the night before.

The grass had been eaten out by the cattle, the ground trampled until it was as bare as a hard, brown dust-bowl.

Stephen, using his ingenuity, found the one place amongst the rocks which the drovers had used and where the water was clear.

"If only a plane would go over," said Alan. "Wonder where the heck they're looking for us? I wasn't so far off route after all."

"They probably combed out this side of the hills yesterday or the day before and have given it up," Stephen said. "They're now hunting over the jungle."

"Which we have vacated," said Tracy with a yawn. "Oh, well, I suppose there's nothing left to do but chase the cattle. When do we leave, Stephen darling?"

"They'd travel five to six miles to-day after a good watering," said Stephen. "That would make them three miles away now. At the slow rate you three have been travelling we wouldn't reach them before nightfall."

"Well, what's stopping us?" said Tracy.

"My ankle," thought Cherry, but she didn't say so.

Stephen rubbed his forehead and looked thoughtfully from Alan to Cherry.

"Can you two make it?" he asked.

Alan looked at Cherry. He knew about her ankle. Obviously Stephen had forgotten it. In a way Alan respected her silence about it but he wasn't going to see her tortured too much. On the other hand, the extra effort might be worth it if it meant a civilised camp for the night.

"Can do, Cherry?" he asked.

She nodded.

"Of course."

"Of course," repeated Tracy. "She's a sound, healthy person, isn't she?"

Night had fallen when they reached the drover's camp. Twenty minutes before they got there they heard the sounds of a raucous old gramophone splitting the warm night air with unearthly sounds.

"He wouldn't carry that thing in his saddle-bags," said Stephen. "Means he's got a truck for his camp gear."

"I hate to say it aloud for fear I break our luck," said Alan. "But I think we're not only found, we've got a conveyance back to civilisation."

"Don't count on it," advised Stephen. "Depends on the size of his plant and whether he can part with it. He'll put his cattle before us."

Stephen spoke with the authority of experience for this is exactly what the drover did do.

He was an elderly man, almost fierce in his bush-whacking hardness and strength, but also hospitable in the same bush-whacking tradition.

Everyone was welcomed to the camp-fire, large hunks of beef were cut from the haunches in the meat-bags hanging under a tree and grilled on the fire over a small iron frame.

Tea was made, cigarettes were dispensed and only then did the old drover think it was time for conversation.

While Tracy reclined on the ground, smoking a cigarette, Alan helped the drover and his camp cook, who later turned out also to be the truck driver, Stephen helped Cherry find a suitable place to bed Peter down for the night and brought her hot water with which to mix more of the dried milk.

"There'll be real red beefsteak juice for Peter this time," he said with a touch of the old teasing note in his voice. "No objections?"

"Of course not," said Cherry. "That was part of his daily diet on the station."

Cherry left the child in its nest in the bushes to go back to the fire to see how the steak was going.

"There's a tin under the piece on the end of the grill, missus," said the drover through an enormous matting of whiskers. "It's catchin' the beef drops fer yer little boy. Guess yer husband kin pick it up outa the fire. Too hot for them white hands of yours."

"My husband?" said Cherry, puzzled, then realised who the drover meant. "Oh, you mean Stephen . . ." She blushed furiously but this was fortunately hidden by the fact the only light on her face was from the flickering flames of the fire. Stephen, she knew, had heard for he had just come forward into the circle round the fire.

"He's not my husband," Cherry said hastily. "He's the little boy's uncle."

"And she is the nursemaid," said Tracy from the ground.

Cherry felt herself go cold. This time Tracy had meant to hurt. There was an unmistakable attack in her voice in spite of the clipped bored tones.

"What you doing with other people's babies?" asked the old drover, flipping over a piece of steak and wiping the back of his hand across his bewhiskered mouth. He straightened up and looked through the flicker of light and shadow at Cherry's slim figure standing irresolute at the edge of the circle of light. She was still dumbfounded at the clear intention to hurt in Tracy's manner.

She was so preoccupied with this mixed feeling of embarrassment and surprise that she did not realise the drover had asked a question.

"Come on, young 'un," he persisted. "Ain't you got a husband uv yer own you got to go round wif *his* children?" He pointed at Stephen.

"The child is not my child. He is my brother's child," Stephen said steadily, bending over to retrieve the tin that had been catching the meat juice under the grill.

Tracy went on smoking her cigarette, and Alan was levering the billies of boiling tea from the fire. Stephen tossed aside the piece of bullock hide the drover had handed him to pick up the tin.

"That can cool there," he said quietly to Cherry. "He's fallen asleep so I think we can have some supper first. We'll give him this when he wakes."

"Ain't you got any babies?" the drover asked, turning to Tracy. "Which uv these fellers is *your* husband?"

"No, and neither," said Tracy. Since he had asked two questions she answered both. "We are two spinsters, not of this parish, travelling with two bachelors. If you're captain of this ship and have got book or bible you can put it all right for us by just saying the word."

"What she mean?" the old drover asked Stephen. Clearly however odd a character he was, he was capable of realising who was the leader of this group of waifs and strays without being told.

"She's talking nonsense because she's tired, like the rest of us. We'll all be more rational by the morning," Stephen replied.

"Guess no one's quite right in the 'ead after a plane crash," the old fellow said. "Tell you what, I got some pills in that medicine tin the Flying Doctor crowd makes us take round these days. Dunno what they're for but they reckons they do yer good whatever yer take 'em for. Never took a pill in me life."

He paused, wiped his whiskers again and pulled his incredibly shabby hat down on to his forehead. He had been lying down with the hat covering his face when the party had stumbled into the camp. True to type it went back on to his head when he sat up. Day or night no bushman travels without his hat.

"Tell you some more," he said. "Them new-fangled things like planes and sich are no good fer crossin' this country. Liable to come down. Now on a good horse and with a decent plant a feller can git him and his six hundred bullocks across anything bar the sea."

Later, sitting round, knees hunched up and large pannikins of tea in front of everyone, they endeavoured to tell the old man something of their troubles over the last few days. It was quite clear that, though they were welcome to his camp hospitality, he was unimpressed by their crash and the subsequent trek through the jungle.

"Thet's what comes uv crossin' territory in airyplanes," he said. "Now you come along wiv me frum now on and I'll git you to Warnock's muster yards inside four days. Split me head in four, if I don't."

"How far back is the nearest station?" Stephen asked.

"That's the Kunder brothers'. Three days' cattle march."

"That means about twelve miles. Could we borrow your truck and take the child back there?"

"You cain't take no one back there, mister. Like I tells you, they's the Kunder brothers. They live like natives and they cain't even read or write. They's got half a million acres and some uv the best cattle in the country and I guess they got nearly as much in the bank or round their dump in milk tins. But they ain't got a decent homestead and you cain't take no child back there. Why, thet there Billy uv mine wouldn't sleep in their dump. An' thet's sayin' a lot."

"Have they got a Transceiver set?"

"One uv them old pedal kind. Runs on a generator. Thet's if you could find anyone home from the run to work the old thing up."

"I'd work it up myself," said Stephen tersely. "We've got to get news back to Yulinga and the airfield at Timor Bay."

"Thet's jes' too bad," said the old drover sorrowfully. "Cause you ain't goin' to git any news to anyone fer four days. You cain't take the truck 'cause my mate, he needs it. Ef you've come from Yulinga I guess yer rich enough to wait. An' my cattle jes won't wait. They'd lose ten pound in weight ef I stood by fer a day in this country. No feed from here to ten miles this side a' Warnock's."

No persuasion, or offering of money, would move the old man. They could come with him, and welcome, but no one was going to borrow the truck.

It transpired he was moving this huge mob of cattle with no more than his offsider who was cook and truck driver, one aboriginal stockman – the man called Billy – and three cattle dogs.

"You ain't the first one says I'm crazy," the old man said affably. "But what you don't know is this. I got a blue heeler that does me instead uv ten men. Hey, Stopper!"

A blue dog, lean, hazel-eyed, flecked with white, sprang up from his place by the fire and stood watching his master's face. His ears were pointed, his slight frame quivering as if ready to spring into action. The drover flicked his fingers and the heeler lay down again.

"I don't hev to talk to thet dog," he said. "I don't even hev to think. He jes' knows."

Stephen smiled. He knew that kind of blue heeler. He was a gold and diamond mine rolled into one as far as a lone drover was concerned.

"The other two dogs is jes' kelpies ordinary. I wouldn't sell 'em fer a hundred pound. But Stopper here does the think' fer the whole plant. And thet goes fer Billy and me offsider too."

The offsider hadn't said a single word and Cherry, listening to all this with fascination, had not yet made up her mind whether the offsider was deaf, dumb or both. Possibly he didn't have to make the effort since Stopper could think for them all.

"Well, thet's thet," said the drover, suddenly deciding there'd been enough conversation for the night.

Tracy was coiled up and probably asleep. Alan had been quietly smoking in silence, listening, like Cherry, while Stephen tried to negotiate with the drover for the loan of the truck if only for a few hours.

"We'd jes' better get a bit of shut-eye," the old man said, standing up. "I'll git me back to me own hole in the ground."

He looked at Stephen and then pushed his finger up under the battered old felt hat and scratched his forehead. He pointed with his thumb at Cherry.

"How you figure yer sleepin'?" he said. "If you ain't married all round, I guess you all got to find some place to sleep elsewhere."

"That's all right," said Stephen quietly. "Cherry will sleep with the child. I imagine Tracy is best left where she is. I think she's asleep already. Alan and I'll move over under the truck . . ."

"*Cherry!* Well, blow me down!" said the old man. "If that ain't a pretty name. Reminds me of them little red things you git summertime in Adelaide. Mighty sweet they are." He bent and peered into Cherry's face. "Yep," he said. "Yer mighty pretty too. Just cain't figure out why you ain't got married, and gotta carry roun' someone else's baby."

Cherry, who had began rather to fall in love with this quaint old drover, smiled up at him. The firelight caught the edges of her teeth and the moist stars in her eyes.

"I haven't tried hard enough," she said laughingly and meaning it as a joke. "Maybe I'll catch someone some day. Then it will be my own baby I carry around."

The drover pointed the stem of his pipe at Stephen.

"Why don't you marry him? If he's one of them Denton brothers from Yulinga, like he says, he's got plenty a' dough. An' he's not so bad-looking either. Fine up-standin' feller."

He looked perplexed and a little injured when Cherry suddenly jumped up and said:

"I ought to wake Peter and feed him now. Otherwise he'll let us know all about it in the middle of the night."

Stephen stood up slowly but with an air of intent.

"I suppose you break camp and start moving before day-light?"

"Me and Billy and the cattle's moving when the first light

comes in. Him . . ." and he pointed at his silent offsider, "he cleans up the camp and takes the gear onta the next camp. Thet's at Mulga's End. You all kin go with him. Room in the back with the gear if you pushes it up. You'd better ask him let the girl and the baby ride up in front. When it comes to them newfangled things like trucks, he's the boss."

Cherry had picked up the tin of meat juice and left the fire circle. Peter's nest in the bushes was not so distant she could not hear the quiet drawling voices of Stephen and the drover continuing discussing plans for the morrow. Alan roused himself from the fireside and came through the shadows towards Cherry.

"Will you be all right for the night, Cherry?" he asked in a quiet voice so as not to alarm Peter who was just waking out of his first sleep.

"Yes, thank you," Cherry said, looking up and smiling.

They were beyond the firelight but an early moon was throwing a white light on to them as they stood near the shelter of the low scrub trees and blue grass bushes.

"It's too warm to worry about coverings," she added. "But if it gets chilly in the night I'll move us both in by the fire." She laughed. "There are far too many of us to matter whether I've got that funny old drover on one side of me and that very silent offsider on the other."

"I'll keep one eye open for you," promised Alan. "I think we'll be all right. My guess is Stephen will keep guard anyway. I understand that awful gramophone has got to be put on again to keep the cattle amused. If the night gets too silent a sudden noise could stampede them."

"I'm too tired to mind," said Cherry.

"Me too," said Alan. "Can I bind your ankle for you before we turn in?"

Cherry shook her head.

"I think I did the best thing for it by walking with it free. It's much better to-night."

Alan hesitated, then said somewhat gruffly :

"Well, good night, Cherry."

"Good night, Alan," she said, smiling at him again.

He half turned but paused. Then he turned back again.

"What do you suppose that old codger meant by trying to marry you and Stephen off? I took a dim view of that. Didn't seem to notice I was in the offing."

"Well, you were round the other side of the camp-fire with Tracy and she was very much asleep against your shoulder. He's so matrimonially minded I think he's already fixed you and Tracy with a gold ring, with or without bell, book, and candle."

"To-morrow night," Alan said with conviction, "I'll fix that camp-fire circle so I'm on the side where you are. And we'll leave Tracy to Stephen."

Cherry smiled.

"Anyhow, it's rather fun, isn't it?" she said. "You know I've never been outback like this before. It makes me think of someone all the time."

"Someone? What someone?" asked Alan, pretending to be alarmed.

Cherry's tone changed subtly.

"Someone who used to live up here, years ago. I often wonder if he did the kind of things I saw Hugh and Stephen Denton doing when I was on Yulinga. And the sort of things this old drover does now . . ."

"Hmm," said Alan, folding his arms and looking glum. "These 'somebodies' in your life. Remind me to investigate them one day, will you?"

"I will," promised Cherry. "Now I'll have to attend to Peter or he'll stampede the cattle before the gramophone has a chance to lull them off with its own brand of din."

"Cheers," said Alan. "And once again, good night."

"Good night, Alan," Cherry said softly and turned away to where Peter was now sitting up, yawning widely and gazing round at his new home with some bewilderment.

"Alan is a dear," Cherry thought as she knelt down to take Peter in her arms. "It's funny but in spite of his being an air-pilot and not a stockman I've got a kind of feeling he's like my father must have been. That's odd. I wonder why."

Then, thinking of this, her thoughts turned back again to the couple down there in the lower latitudes worrying about her whereabouts now.

"Poor darlings," she thought. "When I'm through this I'll go home to them. I promised Dad it would be in a year's time. But somehow, after this, I know they'll want me."

She was sitting cross-legged on the ground with Peter in her arms by this time. She held the tin of warmed meat juice to his lips. Her eyes rested on the sheen the moonlight made of his soft downy head.

"But how," she added, "will I ever bring myself to part with you?"

Peter obligingly swallowed a drop the wrong way and gave himself up to a spasm of coughing. This took Cherry's mind off her divided loyalties long enough to stop worrying about to whom she would devote the rest of her life.

When later she crouched down in the long dried grass with Peter in her arms it was the old drover's injunction to marry and have a child of her own that she thought of.

And the drover had selected Stephen as the prospective candidate.

Cherry thought of Stephen, sitting by the fire, a dark concentrated expression on his face as he tried to persuade the drover to lend them the truck. Suddenly it reminded her of Stephen sitting on the white beach at the foot of the Street of the Pines.

It seemed a long time since she had thought of him that way. The attractive mystery man on the sands had turned first into a taciturn pastoralist and then into the determined leader of their little plane-wrecked crew.

Finally, of course, the drover would have him turn into Cherry's husband.

Cherry, half asleep, gurgled at the thought of the annoyance Stephen must have felt.

She wondered why her own heart felt suddenly sad.

It must be Tracy, she supposed. And of course the knowledge that the Stephens of the world were not for her. She had a father and mother to whom she owed her first, perhaps her only loyalties.

She must stop thinking about prospective husbands, let alone giving her heart away to other people's children.

Nevertheless she drew Peter closer.

An hour later Stephen, walking quietly around the camp to make sure all was well with his responsibilities, saw the moonlight shining on Cherry's face where her chin rested on the little boy's head. She lay, Peter in her arms, curved in a half moon amongst the small trees.

This time he was not amused at the quaint figure Cherry Landin cut.

CHAPTER THIRTEEN

The noise in and about the camp woke Cherry before dawn. The cattle from habit knew they should be on the move. There was a bellowing and stamping in the herd. Billy, the stockman, was galloping out, cracking a stockwhip to round up the mob, heading the leaders in the right direction. Now and again a dog gave a short sharp bark.

The camp-fire was glowing with coals and by this light, helped a little by the false dawn, Stephen could be seen assisting the drover to break camp and saddle the horses.

Cherry, stiff from her sleep on an old rug lent by the drover, could see the men's shadows as they worked with great strength and speed.

The man who was truck driver, offsider and cook, was grilling steak for breakfast.

Cherry got out Peter's tin of dried milk and proceeded to make him a drink.

Alan was the only one who exchanged a word with Cherry as she came to the camp-fire.

"'Morning," he said. "Sleep well? You don't have to answer unless willing. 'Scuse me while I rescue that steak in the coals. As you see, I'm cook's offsider this morning."

Tracy was still rolled in a rug, apparently fast asleep though less than twenty-five yards from where the horses, stamping and rattling their bits, were being saddled at ferocious speed by Stephen and the drover.

"Let Tracy cook and you help the men," Cherry suggested. She sensed that this was how Alan would rather have it.

"Dear child, have you ever lifted one of those saddles? They're made of wood and iron. I'm not joking. That's what these outback fellers use. The old boy has got the strength of ten and by the look of it Stephen can give him another ten man-power."

Cherry retrieved the tin of hot water and began to pour in and mix the milk powder.

"It's good of Stephen to help," she said.

"He's helping himself. He's going to ride back to that station they were talking about last night. He didn't let the old chap go to bed until he'd promised him the use of two horses, if he couldn't have the truck."

"How far is it? Twelve miles, I think they said. What does he want two horses for?"

She felt a drop in her spirits at the prospect of losing Stephen from their party. She knew they were all safe at last but somehow five would now only be four and the Jack of Hearts would be missing.

Heavens! What made her think of that? Well, Stephen was rather a colourful figure. He was very nice when he wasn't being superior and the archetype of the great landowning class. Maybe she had always liked the Jack of Hearts when she had played rummy with Dad on winter evenings, because that was just what the Jack of Hearts was. Nice, but rich and unobtainable when you held in your hand five trumps of another suit.

Alan retrieved more grilled steak from the frame on the coals, put it on a tin plate and covered it with another plate.

"It seems we eat as much steak for breakfast as most families would eat in a year," he said to Cherry. "That's why the drover and his team are so tough. Steak only for diet. By the way, notice I put Peter's meat tin under the grill to catch the beef drops."

"Yes, thank you very much. You are a darling, Alan, and I guess Peter will be grateful too."

" If he ever sees me again. Stephen's taking him back with him to that station."

Cherry nearly dropped the tin of milk.

" Stephen and who else?" she said.

" Tracy, when she wakes up."

Cherry poured the heated milk from the tin into a plastic cup and as she did so her hands trembled.

" No," she said to herself. " No, no, no!"

The drover had said that station wasn't fit for habitation. The owners were rough men and lived in a shanty. Even the native stockman wouldn't sleep there. The drover had said that. It might be dirty. It might be ridden with . . . well, ridden with anything.

And Tracy looking after Peter!

" Oh no, Mr. Stephen Denton. You've got another think coming if you think I'll give up Peter to Tracy's care. Why, his own parents didn't trust him to Tracy. They sent me, but *me*, to take him to Timor Bay to have his injections. And that was in a civilised plane to a civilised place. And what's more Tracy was going too. But they didn't leave Peter to Tracy. They gave him to *me*."

She did not answer Alan and he watched her go out of the light of the fire into the shadows with Peter's early morning drink. As dawn came stealing, a grey misty light over the plain and into the clump of trees in which the party was camped, he saw her sitting, her back slightly bent, with Peter in her arms, feeding him from the cup. Her face was turned to the child's face.

" That's hurt her," he said to himself. " But I thought I'd break it to her first. She'd have found it too hard to take direct from Stephen. He doesn't soften his blows."

Tracy stirred, unrolled herself and sat up and stretched. Presently she came, still half asleep, towards the fire.

Alan gave her a few minutes and then broke to her the plans for the day.

" Me ride on one of those rocking-horses saddles? I bet that's what they use. And Peter too? Huh! Then Stephen can carry him."

Cherry had come to the fire for Peter's next course, and

143

Alan handed her the tin of meat juice which he had already retrieved from the fire by means of a long fork and a piece of hide. She looked up as Tracy spoke, stood irresolute a minute as if she would say something, but then changed her mind. She went back to the child.

The offsider had finished his share of steak grilling and was now throwing all available utensils, the rugs and other camp gear in the back of his truck. Cherry, carrying Peter, crossed over to him.

Billy the black stockman had come in by this time for his breakfast; hunks of left-over beef were given to the dogs and Stephen and the drover now went to the camp to get their share of billy tea and steak.

It was nearly daylight and the plain stretched away to the north and west, an eerie sea of grey, lifeless grass. Beside them was the clump of trees and beyond that the low hills they had crossed yesterday.

Somewhere north-east of that was the jungle country they had left such a short time ago. Somehow, at this moment that camp in the jungle, silent and empty except for the plane wreckage and the gear they had left behind, seemed to Cherry like a lost heaven and a home to which there was no return.

Why hadn't she known in those few days that *there* had been perfect happiness. Now, back on the fringe of the civilised world she was faced again with all the problems of those who have rights and those who have no rights.

There in the jungle camp her care of Peter had been a duty required of her. Here it was a privilege of which Stephen would now deprive her.

" Please," she said to the truck driver, " when do you move out? Before the cattle or after?"

" Before and after, missus. I takes the first load on to Mulga's End, six miles on. Then I give the cattle a wide circle and comes back the southern end of 'em for the rest of the gear and for you fellers."

" Have you had your breakfast?" Cherry asked with careful politeness.

" Yeah. I always feeds self first. Then I can go when I'm good an' ready."

" Are you good and ready yet?"

" For the first load? Jes' on. 'Nother five minutes."

" Do you mind if I sit up in the cab till you are ready, please?"

The truck driver shrugged.

" You kin sit any place you like, lady. You can even come first trip with me if you likes. It's not so bad at Mulga's End. A good lake and a decent feed for the bullocks."

" I'd like to come," said Cherry. " But please don't say anything to the others just now."

The truck driver pushed his finger under his ancient felt hat and scratched his head.

" I guess it's all right, if you says so . . ."

" They might all want to come first trip," said Cherry. " And you haven't got room, have you?"

" No darn' fear I haven't. You jes' get up there in the cab an' not a word to anyone."

Cherry looked over her shoulder but no one at the camp was looking her way at the moment. She walked round the side of the truck, took Peter's tin of milk and plastic cup from inside her blouse and put them on the cab seat, then hoisted herself up, still holding the boy.

As she sat there and waited she told herself she was mad. This way was no real escape. The truck only went six miles to Mulga's End. But somehow doing it this way was better than arguing with Stephen. One thing she was certain, no one, *no one*, was going to take Peter from her except by brute force; and that would have to be exerted with considerable effort.

It was rough driving in that truck for there was no real track for wheels. They went over hummocks of grass, flat boulders of rock, deep indentations in the ground. The truck swayed from side to side and Peter, fresh from his long sleep in the open air, squealed with delight.

Cherry held him tightly.

What, she wondered, was the law of child custody? Would the law regard her as the right custodian since Hugh Denton and his wife had given Peter to her? Mrs. Denton had put

Peter in her arms at the homestead and Hugh Denton had handed him up to her in the plane. They had given their child into her care. But had they? Hadn't they said Stephen was going to Timor Bay, and that Stephen needed her help?

All right, he needed her help. Then why was he taking Tracy to that awful place twelve miles back on the stock route? Why Tracy? Because he loved her! That, Cherry supposed, was excuse enough.

All right for Stephen and Tracy but not good enough for Peter.

Cherry, so deeply immersed in these thoughts, didn't notice the silence of the truck driver or the fearfulness of the track. She didn't even notice how much Peter was enjoying himself.

She came out of this deep and melodramatic state of mind when the truck driver suddenly braked and they came to a stop. He leaned sideways out of the cab and looked back along the track.

"The other feller's coming," he said, pulling in his head and looking at Cherry. "The tall one what owns the baby."

Cherry said nothing. She let her chin sink down on Peter's head and there she waited in silence until the horseman came alongside. She stared straight ahead and did not turn her eyes when Stephen's head and shoulders appeared in the glassless window of the truck. She knew, however, that he was not smiling and that his dark grey eyes were almost black with anger.

He swung himself from the horse, slung its bridle over the exposed radiator cap of the ancient vehicle and with a slow and purposeful tread walked back to the cabin door. He pulled it open with a jerk.

"Get out, Cherry!" he said. "This has wasted several hours of precious time."

She turned her head and looked at him now. Her eyes were quite clear.

"And walk back?" she asked. "You've only brought one horse, Stephen. When you were going to take Tracy, with Peter, you had borrowed two horses."

"Very well," he said evenly. "You can stay in the truck. Peter goes with me."

Cherry shook her head.

"You said we had to stay together in twos. One man and one girl."

"You've got the truck driver. You're safe."

"I'm sure I am. And so is Peter – with me."

Stephen spoke very wildly. "Peter is my nephew," he said. "I am taking him back to the nearest point of civilisation. He is an infant, and it is my duty to take charge of him."

The truck driver rolled himself a cigarette, pulled his hat down, almost over his eyes, and gazed with a bored expression into the sameness of the track that lay ahead.

"Well, I don't think that place back there is civilised," Cherry said conversationally. "Of course, if I went with Peter I would be a good judge of that."

Now she smiled, guilelessly and straight into Stephen's eyes.

"Tracy doesn't like rocking-horse saddles . . . she said so . . . she doesn't like holding Peter. And the only kind of civilisation Tracy can recognise with an expert's eyes is the stage of Covent Garden. Preferably with Dame Margot Fonteyn on it."

A muscle moved in Stephen's cheek. He dropped his foot from the step of the truck and reached in his pocket for cigarettes. There were none. Cherry took what she called her "bribe packet" from the pocket of her shirt and opening it took out one cigarette and handed it to him.

"You've forgotten rationing days went out with the finding of the drover's camp," she said sweetly.

Stephen was silent, looking at her as if he hadn't made up his mind whether to drag Peter from her arms and leave her in the truck, or smack her.

"You can smell it if you don't want to smoke it," Cherry said cajolingly. "They say that helps when you're trying to give up the vice."

Stephen took the cigarette from her, and the truck driver,

without turning his head or saying a word, handed him a box of matches over Cherry's head.

Stephen drew on the cigarette, looked down at the ground and then through slitted eyes out across the plain.

It was daylight and the sun, rising in the east, was reflected in the pink carpet of grass to the west.

He looked back at Cherry. His eyes all but relented.

"All right," he said. "You win. Move over while I tie the horse on the back of the truck."

"Where you goin' now, mister?" asked the truck driver

"You turn round and drive us back to the camp. Swing wide of the cattle. I'm paying you ten pounds for your trouble."

"Ten pounds for two miles?" said Cherry, indignant.

Stephen tied the horse to the tailboard of the truck and climbed in beside Cherry.

"That," said Stephen dryly, "is what it cost me for you to run away."

"Suits me," said the truck driver and, pushing his hat to the back of his head, put the truck into gear and let go the brake. He swung wide out from the track and now the bumping was worse than before.

"Pretty bad," said Stephen, looking down at her when they gave one particularly bad lurch over a miniature canyon in the middle of their way. It seemed to give him pleasure.

"Not so bad now," said Cherry airily. "I've got you to bump against. Before it was the cab door I kept hitting." She looked at Stephen. "But that wasn't quite so hard," she admitted.

The cattle were beginning to string out when they got back to the camp.

The drover was on horseback somewhere out on the wing and Billy the stockman was on the near side. The blue heeler, Stopper, was bringing up the rear.

Tracy and Alan were drinking tea over the near dead fire. There was another horse, an enormous brown animal with a white star on his forehead and a long flowing mane, tied to a tree limb.

"What goes on?" said Tracy, looking at Cherry as if she was something impertinent that had turned up uninvited at a society tea-party. "You eloping with yet another man?"

"You mean the truck driver?" said Cherry innocently. "Well, actually he's the first. Unless you count Peter a man."

"Have some tea, darling," Tracy said to Stephen, holding up a billy of black tea. "And please explain what happens next."

Cherry put Peter down on the ground where he immediately began to scrabble around for sticks with which to play. She, herself, took her comb from the hip pocket of her slacks and began to comb her fringe down flat.

Stephen took the billy from Tracy and poured some of the tea into a plastic cup.

"You go in the truck with Alan," Stephen said quietly. "He'll look after you. Right?" He looked up inquiringly at Alan.

The pilot nodded his head.

"Right as rain," he said.

"Pleasant if we had some rain," said Tracy. "Apart from being able to wash ourselves clean Cherry could lick that fringe down into form. It has been unco-operative ever since we landed on the treetops in that plane."

Cherry, standing above Peter so that no one could take him from her, her feet a little apart, went on combing her hair and said nothing.

"Cherry and I'll go on to Kunders' place. They've a Transceiver set and if they haven't motor transport a station that size will have a dozen horses in the home paddock." He paused, looked up at Cherry. "Tea?" he asked, coldly polite, holding out the cup.

"Thank you," said Cherry.

She took the cup but did not move her guardian-like stance above Peter. She hadn't had any breakfast so standing on her dignity and politely declining the tea wasn't going to get her anywhere.

If only someone would offer her a good charcoal-burned

steak too! She might swallow her pride enough to take a peck at it.

Alas, during her two-mile trip there in the truck and two-mile trip back the camp had been cleared and packed except for the billies of tea and the cups they were holding.

No one had noticed – not even Alan Donnelly – that Cherry had not had breakfast. Well, she had no one to blame for that state of affairs but herself. She drank the tea with pleasure.

"And Cherry goes with you?" Tracy asked askance, looking round Stephen at Cherry.

"Cherry will look after Peter," Stephen said. After a pause he added, "She is more used to him. I feel I must put Peter first, Tracy."

"Have you ever ridden on one of those iron frame saddles, Cherry?" Tracy asked sweetly.

Cherry shook her head.

"I haven't ridden on any saddle," she said. "But I'll get there. After being plane-wrecked in a jungle I can take anything."

"Oh sure," said Tracy affably. "But I promise you you won't take anything, not even a kind word or a fillet cut for dinner, after you get there. You won't be fit."

Cherry had put her comb back in her hip pocket and over the rim of her cup her eyes met Alan Donnelly's. He winked at her.

"At least you won't have to walk on a lame ankle," he said. "That ought to be something."

Stephen's eyes went to Cherry's feet but she quickly moved her left foot, the injured one, behind the right foot.

"So long as Peter is safe——" she said equably.

"We ought to get back to Mulga's End before nightfall," Stephen said to Alan. "With any luck we'll find a car or utility at Kunders' Station. The important thing is that I can get through to the world on that Transceiver set. I think we owe Hugh and Betty that."

"And the rest of our folks," Alan said.

"Funny," Cherry thought, swallowing the last of her tea and shaking the drains out on the ground. "On a walkabout like this, one forgets that each person has 'other folks.' Everyone has, of course. I wonder who Alan is worrying about. He never says anything. But then I don't either, do I?"

In some ways, Cherry thought, they were all very uninhibited. She herself emptying the drains of her cup on to the ground, for instance. And combing her hair like that too. Was that just shaking off the shibboleths of convention or was she measuring up to Tracy, Tracy's way?

On the other hand they were all buttoned up in knots inside. Her own worry for her parents, Alan's comment about "our folks" were good examples.

What private woes and worries did Tracy really cover up behind that manner of the bored sophisticate? If she was really in love with Stephen, and really intended to marry him, she at least had him on hand to share her worries.

Cherry stooped and picked up Peter. His new plaything, a fistful of sticks, had to be gently eased from his grubby hand, a piece of wet cloth had to be found to wipe those same hands and his little shining eager face.

Another breakfast had to be made for him and meantime the last remains of the camp were cleaned up by Stephen and Alan.

The truck driver remained aloof, except for the last of the drover's plant which it was his duty to assemble in a pile ready for his return trip. His manner seemed to say for him – I wish you people would hurry up.

CHAPTER FOURTEEN

Eventually all was ready and the truck started away with Tracy in the cab and Alan sitting on top of the gear in the back. He waved a nonchalant hand of farewell to Stephen and Cherry standing beside the two horses that were to carry them in the opposite direction.

"See you for dinner," he called. His eyes, smiling ruefully, lingered on Cherry. "Chin up, girl," was his last piece of advice. "Half a dozen hours and we'll meet again."

Cherry smiled back as she waved. Stephen turned and looked at her a moment.

"I should have made you go with Alan," he said. "I don't know what's come over me that I start having my decisions altered by a small piece of womanhood like you."

"Not me," said Cherry. "It was Peter. Otherwise I assure you it would have been fun to ride up on the back of the truck like that." She put her head a little on one side and pursed her lips. "Consider my riding off with you on that great big horse the stern call of duty."

Stephen rubbed the back of his forefinger across his chin. He looked thoughtfully from Cherry to Peter, again scrabbling for sticks where he sat on the ground.

"'And a little child shall lead them,'" he quoted. Then his face relaxed and he smiled. "Strange how a whole world will turn the opposite way when an infant's welfare is involved."

"If you and I are the whole world," said Cherry, "then we'd better turn the opposite way at once. Otherwise I won't be able to keep that appointment for dinner with Alan at Mulga's End."

Stephen went to the tree where the horses were hitched and led the two animals round to stand side by side. He adjusted the stirrup leathers of Cherry's mount then looked over the saddle at her.

"We call a temporary truce then?" he said, his dark grey eyes asking a question, his mouth eased in that small, amused smile that always made Cherry think he was laughing at her.

She nodded.

"How do I get up?" she asked. "Will you hand Peter up to me?"

"Yes."

She already had Alan's carrying-bag across her shoulder and Stephen came round to the left side of her mount and held the stirrup for her.

"Put your weight on the ball of the foot," he said. "And spring up from your right."

Mounting a horse looked so easy for other people but
herry didn't have any illusions as to how badly she might
) it herself. She concentrated on what Stephen told her
do. The stirrup iron was high because the horse was big.
e felt as if she had got her left knee somewhere in the
alm of her chin when she put her foot in the iron.

She glanced at Stephen, expecting to see him laughing
her, but his face was concentrated and serious. With a
ng of remorse Cherry realised that whatever else his
ults, he was too gallant to do that. His manners to the
dies, though distant, were always chivalrous.

"Hand on pommel and grip," he said. "Now *up*."

Unexpectedly his own hand was under her right foot
she sprang and she sailed up into the saddle of this
ormous horse like a bird.

She could not help the look of surprised amazement on
r face to find herself sitting there, on top of the world,
th feet nicely placed in the stirrup irons and Stephen
anding down there on the earth making no attempt to
de his expression of ironic amusement. It was not a muscle
at was moving in his cheek now, it was his tongue.

Then he turned away, bent down and picked up Peter.
"Ready?" he said. "Up. Sit steady while you fit his legs
the bag. Good."

He held the mount at the cheek strap while Cherry adjusted
ter into a comfortable position.

"You are now mounted on a packhorse," Stephen said
an enlightening manner. "He won't gallop or canter
t he just might trot if he gets cantankerous. You can
ld the reins and otherwise forget about him. He'll follow
e and I'll keep the pace down. Right?"

An old packhorse! And she had thought she was going
rth on a stockman's charger!

How Stephen must really be laughing behind that curious
pressionless glaze of his eyes.

He did have nice eyes, though. It was a pity they always
d the wrong expression in them. Well, nearly always.

Cherry sighed. She nodded.

" When you get tired – and you will—" Stephen cautioned "I'll take over Peter. Now, we'll get away."

With considerable envy Cherry watched Stephen go up into the saddle of the other mount in an effortless way. As he sat a moment and looked round the camp to make sure they had left nothing behind – he had the waterbag with him and food rations in his saddle-bag – Cherry looked at his straight back, the easy way his feet hung long in the stirrups. There was nothing ramrod about him and he looked so easy he might have been born in the saddle.

He glanced across at Cherry.

"Right?" he said again.

She nodded.

He touched a rein and his horse walked forward, out of the clump of trees on to the cattle track which was well churned from yesterday's travelling bullocks. Cherry's mount rocked and swayed into motion behind him and it didn't take her five minutes to discover why Tracy had given in to the change of arrangements so readily and why Stephen had worn that slightly amused smile that had seemed to say . . . "You asked for it. Now you've got it."

Peter, of course, was thrilled. He was on a real live rocking-horse and in addition the world from this elevation had achieved a new wonder for him. He kept turning his face up to Cherry to make sure she registered just how remarkable a thing it was to be alive. Then he would heave a fatuous sigh of satisfaction and return his gaze to the splendours of a grassless plain.

How simple are the joys of a child, thought Cherry, as she rocked this way and that; backwards and forwards, the horse's feet clopping along at a pace that would take them all day to-day and possibly to-morrow to travel twelve miles.

She understood perfectly what Tracy had meant – or was it Alan? – by a wood and iron-framed saddle. Certainly there was leather under her but everywhere else – across her instep, against her back, thrusting at her forelegs, were iron bars and wooden barriers. Or so it seemed to Cherry.

Meantime her inside organs rattled around like peas in pod.

Each time Stephen glanced around she jerked up her head and put on an expression of nonchalance. She could never have counted the number of times that expression arrived on her face only after an uninhibited grimace of pain.

They hadn't gone very far when they reined in. Stephen swung his leg over his saddle and slid to the ground. He came back to Cherry, the reins of his own mount over his arm. The packhorse automatically stopped. Its manner indicated it was not likely to take another step forward.

Stephen was too polite to smile. He rubbed his cheek with the back of his finger and then said :

"Now do you think you could trust Peter to me?"

So he had punished her. She would never forgive him out of this she could say nothing at the moment. She merely nodded, defeated.

She loosened Peter from his shoulder bag and handed him down to Stephen who set the child on the ground. He now held up his arms to Cherry.

"Do I get off?" she said.

He nodded. Again that infuriating half smile flitted around his mouth.

"The big bay is quite docile and more comfortable to ride," he said.

"But you——"

"Never mind about me. I can ride a packhorse and make him go too. I'll give you a demonstration in a minute."

Cherry loosened her right foot from the stirrup. She would have liked to disdain Stephen's waiting arms but she knew she couldn't do that. She wanted to fall into them, never leave them, and certainly never mount another horse again as long as she lived.

She put her hands on Stephen's shoulders, meaning to elevate herself lightly from the saddle and descend to the ground as easily as she had gone up into the saddle — with his help.

Instead, as she leaned forward, she quite literally fell

into his arms. He lifted her free of the saddle and th
near stirrup iron and lowered her gently to the groun
He held her as he gave her feet time to find the groun
and settle on them firmly.

Suddenly her eyes were full of tears because she coul
not help the fact that she had to lean against him. Fo
a minute she was helpless and had no balance.

Stephen looked down at her.

She was still in his arms and she had to bend her hea
forward so the knuckles of her hand would wipe the tear
from her eyes for her. That way he could see only th
top of her head, thank goodness.

Nevertheless, when she shook her head as if to shake awa
cobwebs from her eyes and lifted it, trying for dignity an
even a touch of hauteur, it was to find Stephen's eyes kindly

"Some people have to learn the hard way, Cherry," h
said gently.

He let her free herself from his arms.

"I guess Tracy learned when she was a child," he added
"She had the advantage of you. Hence her docile willing
ness to go ahead in the truck."

"I suppose I asked for it," agreed Cherry, turning t
see where Peter had got to. "But you might have told me
Oh, Stephen! *Look!*"

For a moment Cherry forgot the awful pain it had cos
her to turn round. He hand went out involuntarily t
Stephen's arm.

A dozen feet away Peter, up on his feet, was walking crazily
but determinedly towards them. His tongue was between hi
teeth, his eyes were wide open with astonishment at hi
own cleverness.

"One-two-three-four-five——" Cherry was breathlessly
counting.

On the eighth step Peter, satisfied with his day's work
sank to the ground, gazed up at them, and beamed.

The cobwebs were back in Cherry's eyes.

"Oh, *Peter!*" she cried.

She took two steps towards him and sank on the ground

beside him. She picked up one of his hands, then turned back helplessly to Stephen.

"I don't think I can get up again," she said.

Stephen was standing looking at the pair of them, the girl and the child, one kneeling and the other sitting on the ground. There was nothing all around them except a waste of treeless, grass-hummocked plain broken here and here by stony outcrops. Away to the north-east was the blue shadow of the edge of the jungle country.

Stephen came over to them and gave Cherry a hand to help her rise.

"I've got a fine pair of you on my hands," he said. "One who won't stop walking now he's started and the other who can't because she took to horseback. They'd better have some motor transport across there on that station."

Cherry straightened herself slowly.

"It would have been better to have brought Tracy, after all."

"I accept your apology in the same handsome spirit it is offered," Stephen said dryly. Then added more kindly, "My decisions are based on some knowledge of people's capabilities, Cherry. But I didn't underrate your care of Peter. Please don't think that. With Tracy I would have looked after Peter's welfare; she would have ridden the distance without undue trouble."

"But Tracy wasn't willing," Cherry thought, though she could not say this.

"Now you've got to do both — look after me and Peter," Cherry said, aloud.

"Exactly," said Stephen.

"Tell me what to do and I'll help myself."

"Good. We'll get you up on the bay first. I'll hand you Peter, then when I'm mounted I'll come alongside and you can hand him to me. Right?"

"Right," said Cherry. She was beginning to like this word "right" of Stephen's. It sort of turned doing things into a team effort.

Well, that's what they were now. A team. She would

have to carry her share. Nobody was any good in a team who had to be carried by others.

With much gritting of teeth, jutting of a bottom lip and grim determination Cherry walked across to the waiting horse without a grimace and as naturally as possible. Again Stephen held the stirrup for her and gave her a leg up. Again, with teeth gritted, Cherry sprang up into the air and into the saddle without flopping back into Stephen's arms. Once there she sat up straight, the balls of her feet firmly pressed on to the stirrup irons.

" I shall not so much as wince once again," she promised herself.

Stephen picked up Peter and handed him to her. Meantime he took the shoulder bag himself.

" Never can tell how much the little tyke will wriggle," he said.

Oddly enough, even on the packhorse Stephen managed to look like a good horseman on a good mount. Cherry, surprised, noticed that he didn't put his right foot in the stirrup. He left it lying across the pommel of the saddle in a " look easy " fashion.

" Don't you ride with both feet?" Cherry asked, curious, as he drew beside her and took Peter from her. He fitted Peter comfortably into his seat, pulled the child's linen hat down on his forehead, then reached in his shirt pocket for the makings of cigarettes which the drover had left for him in the camp.

" If you watch closely," said Stephen casually, "you will see that I bump less, can ride easily and at the same time carry a child and roll myself a cigarette . . . all at the same time, if I ride this way." Then he said by way of a joke to ease their relationship. " Besides, my right leg needs a rest. You go ahead. This time I'll be the lubra."

Startled, Cherry realised that that was just what she must have looked like to Stephen earlier. The man riding daringly ahead, the lubra following on the old nag, the baby in a sling. What a picture! Of course, it had a domestic tang to it, in aboriginal fashion, but all the same it was the picture of subservient woman.

She decided not to be offended because Stephen was now, vigorously and with a smile of amusement on his face, doing exactly the same thing.

They rode several miles this way. As the pace was not much more than a walk with occasional bursts of trotting and even a canter or two Cherry was much more comfortable on the big stockhorse. True, the iron-framed saddle was hard, her back ached and other parts of her, notably her insteps where the stirrup iron cut into her, were sore but she had ceased to feel all her insides being rattled about like loose works in a shake-box.

Getting off later, and walking about, would be painful, she knew. But at least she would be whole and her body would be expected to be all in one piece. And she would keep a stiff upper lip. On that she was determined.

It was nearly midday by the position of the sun in the heavens when Stephen called a halt.

He came up beside Cherry and handed her Peter, slid off the packhorse and then took the child from her.

"Don't get off till I've put Peter some place safe from the horses' feet," he warned.

Cherry had learned wisdom so she did not, this time, take the law into her own hands and demonstrate her independence by trying to dismount herself.

There was only one way and that was to be the least possible trouble.

She meekly sat on the horse until, Peter safely put down in the shade of some scrub, Stephen came towards her. Again he put up both arms to take her weight. Cherry, everything under control, unconscious of the determined line of her mouth and the sudden concentrated expression in her dark blue eyes, allowed her weight to come easily towards him. He lifted her to the ground as if she were weightless.

He held her steady for a few minutes. Had Cherry only known, her eyes had exactly the same expression as small Peter's had had when he was essaying his first few walking steps. She was concentrating on that stiff upper lip so much that this time she failed to see the expression in Stephen own eyes.

He drew in the corners of his mouth and dropped h hands, as he saw that she stood steady, and turned awa He began to take their lunch – damper and cold grill steak – from the saddle-bags. Peter's inevitable tin of mi and the waterbag were taken from the hooks on the packhor saddle.

" We'll sit in the shade over there," he indicated with h head. He had his back to Cherry as she walked stiffly b determinedly towards the scrub. He did not turn round un he knew she was safely sitting down beside the child.

Cherry did not acknowledge this gallantry aloud but her heart she saluted him.

Oddly it made her a little sad. Half of her, the sil half, was beginning to fall for him all over again.

It was no good pretending that the Cherry who was inexperienced ex-schoolgirl had not fallen for him when h was a lone mysterious figure sitting on that golden beach many thousand miles away. That mad " crush " had di appeared, she told herself, when he had come to the hous had inwardly laughed at her parents and her home, ar anyhow had turned out to be a rich and unattainable statio owner.

Then, of course, he had been difficult on and off ever sinc She assured herself of this. In addition he was born an bred to the Tracys of this world, not to small-time governess who turned out to be no more than nursemaids.

Alan Donnelly was different.

Cherry had a pang of remorse when she remembered Ala Donnelly. She felt as if she had suddenly been caught defec ing from a point of honour. It was she and Alan who ha been the good companions in all this strange time since th plane was wrecked. Alan had been thoughtful, kind, amuse and amusing. He had hidden his troubles from the other He had borne himself with dignity since he had not only bee the pilot of the plane that had crashed but had also s immediately been superseded in authority by Stephen.

"There is as much character in serving as directing," Cherry thought.

She would not let Stephen do this to her — make her feel a sudden exulting pride in the fact her heart bowed a little to his occasional gallantries.

Stephen had everything. He didn't have to have all the hearts too. Tracy's heart was enough surely, since Tracy, in his eyes, had no faults.

As Stephen brought the waterbag and the saddle-bag to the shade in the scrub Cherry's eyes wandered away to that north-eastern horizon where the blue shadow that must be the edge of the timbered country still lay, a smudge on the horizon. How happy they had been there!

How sad to think of that derelict camp lying alone in the clearing, waiting for four people and a child to come home. Four people and a child who would never come now. They were heading for a station, motor transport, and civilisation.

Cherry supposed that in her heart that camp in the clearing would now remain the Shangri-La of her dreaming — a place where once nothing mattered and where there was no other world but huge trees, fallen logs, a wall of vine and four or five miles away a lily-strewn lake where birds came from hundreds of miles for their evening swim.

"Why so quiet?" Stephen asked, looking at Cherry closely. He was trying to gauge how badly knocked out she was by that ride. It was a ride that was nothing to him and with Tracy he could have made it in a quarter of the time but he nevertheless knew that any first ride is a trying experience for a novice and this one with those iron-backed saddles had been doubly hard on a girl.

Cherry had one hand on Peter and was unconsciously patting his arm. Peter, tired, had lain back on the ground, had put two fingers in his mouth, decided he had outgrown that piece of babyishness now he could walk, and was closing his eyes instead. If they didn't hurry up and feed him, his expression said, he'd fall asleep instead of eating.

"I was thinking of the jungle," Cherry said, her eyes a little dreamy, coming back to Stephen's face as he bent over the saddle-bags. "It was rather nice there, wasn't it? We did have fun——"

"Very nice," said Stephen noncommittally. "Including the pythons."

"Oh, I'd forgotten the pythons. There's always a catch even in the nicest things, isn't there?"

Stephen had extracted the plastic mugs and was pouring water into one of them.

"What was so nice about it?"

"The company for one thing," said Cherry. "I wonder what Alan and Tracy are doing now?"

"Not mixing dried milk for small boys, that's for certain," said Stephen.

"Oh, I'm sorry," exclaimed Cherry. "I'd even forgotten Peter. How dreadful——"

She reached forward and Stephen handed her the tin of milk with the cup of water.

"The world generally seems to be well forgotten for love," Stephen said as he opened the second saddle-bag. "Is that why you fell in love with the jungle? That way you shut out other claims?"

"What other claims?" asked Cherry, stirring in the milk with a stick.

"You have people, friends, commitments down south. Being shut away in a jungle shuts away the south, doesn't it?"

"Yes," said Cherry contritely. "I suppose it does."

In truth it wasn't very kind of her to be thinking nostalgically of a camp in the jungle when her parents were still probably crazed with anxiety.

She bent over and roused Peter and drew him into her arms. She held the cup to his lips. As she did so she looked up.

"Don't let's rest too long, Stephen. Somehow we've got to get to that Transceiver set as quickly as possible. I can't bear to think of people worrying."

"How do you feel?"

"It doesn't matter how I feel," said Cherry doggedly. "We've got to get to that station. If you'll hurry I'll promise not to hold you up again. I'll even ride that old packhorse——"

" A reminder of your people down south has certainly had a salutary effect on your energy," Stephen said dryly. " A minute ago I thought you'd follow Peter's example and go to sleep."

" I'll sleep when I get through on that Transceiver set," said Cherry firmly.

" To the man down south?"

" To the man down south," said Cherry.

Peter finished his drink and was put back on the leafy ground to get on with his sleep. Stephen handed Cherry her share of damper and cold beef. They sat eating in silence.

Stephen half closed his eyes against the glare of the sun as he looked out across the plain.

It was hard on a girl, he supposed, when she found her heart divided between two men. Just how much had Alan Donnelly played the handsome gallant while he, Stephen, and Tracy had been away hunting those two days Alan and Cherry had been left alone at the camp?

And how much was she attached to this other man down south?

He turned his head a little and looked at Cherry where she had leaned her head back against the slim trunk of a scrub gum. Her eyes were closed.

He sat watching her for a minute, his face expressionless, then he turned back to look across the plain, a shadow in his eyes.

A ball of brown dust was bowling towards them from the south. It was coming along that cattle track.

It was not a willy-willy, because a willy-willy was spiral and it danced. This was a ball and it raced.

Stephen sat upright, his eyes slitted, the shadow gone. Presently he spoke softly between half-closed lips.

" Cherry," he said. " Open your eyes. You'll see God's greatest creation coming towards you. A man in a motor car."

Cherry opened her eyes and sat up. She stared unbelievingly at the big overlanding car that was materialising out of its enveloping cloak of dust.

Stephen had not moved. He sat, his knees drawn up and his elbows resting on them. He took out the tin of tobacco and papers the drover had given him and began slowly to roll a cigarette.

"Now," he said, without raising his eyes, "you will be able to get on to that boy friend of yours without delay. If my sight is right the sun is catching a certain gleaming object rearing itself up from the back fin of that car. It's a radio rod."

"Boy friend?" said Cherry dazedly. She blinked her eyes. "Boy friend?" She looked down at the sleeping Peter. "That's the only boy friend I've got. I wish he was truly mine."

Stephen unlooped himself and stood up. He held out his hand to help her rise. Just as Cherry had forgotten she held Stephen's arm when she watched Peter walk, now she forgot she held his hand, tightly, as they stood side by side and the great dust-covered overlander skidded to a surprised stop at the side of the track.

CHAPTER FIFTEEN

Everything that happened in the next twenty-four hours kaleidoscoped into a rush of events.

The owner of the overlander was one of the Kunder brothers from Kunder Station. He was a big, thickset man, roughly dressed but with a bush-whacker's heart of gold.

"Knock me down!" he said. "That lost plane! An' you're all alive. Ringin' bells! That darn radio has done nothin' this last four days but yabber yabber about that plane."

Time was urgent but not too urgent for a cup of tea. Alex Kunder might not have been able to read or write but there was nothing he didn't know about motor mechanics, radio mechanics and carrying a travelling food box in the boot of his enormous car.

With great pride he demonstrated how he had built his car by picking up an old body here, an old engine there, engine parts from anyone who came through his station. And similarly with everything that went to make a two-way radio set for this monstrous, mechanical pride of his heart.

While Stephen raided the food box and Cherry, now adept, built a small camp-fire to boil the billy, Alex Kunder endeavoured to demonstrate how he had made everything himself and how he'd made everything work.

"Good heavens!" said Stephen, interrupting at one stage while he put fistfuls of beautiful tea-leaves into the billy, then strung a gum twig across the mouth of the billy to prevent the subsequent brew from tasting too smoky. "With twenty thousand head of cattle on that run, why don't you buy yourself a car? Or half a dozen for that matter? Why make one?"

"'Cause then I wouldn't have made it meself," replied the puzzled station owner. "What's the good of anything you can't make yourself?"

Stephen looked at him across the fire which was now springing well into action.

"I think you've got something there," he said thoughtfully. Then he turned teasingly to Cherry. "This young lady seems to prefer a self-made home in a jungle to a man-made one in more civilised places."

Cherry smiled back at him through the smoke.

"I would but *you* wouldn't," she said. "You like the last thing in what's what. Look at that house down there in the Street of the Pines. All modern conveniences. And of course glamour and sophistication in your womenfolk." She turned to their rescuer. "Please, Mr. Kunder, does that radio send out as well as receive? Could you work it for us?"

"Just getting around to that, lady. Besides, I gotta let my brother know what I found. Ringin' bells, I found some funny things on this station in my time but I certainly never found a man and a girl and a kid before. Not all together and not white, anyway."

He got into his car and began to dicker with dials that

165

no one would have known were dials if Alex Kunder hadn't mentioned the fact.

Stephen abandoned the tea-making to Cherry and got into the car beside him.

What a strange pair they made, Cherry thought. Stephen, even though his clothes had been spoiled by jungle hunting, his shoes muddied and scratched, his hat rendered almost shapeless, still looked distinguished. Alex Kunder, unshaven, not scrupulously bathed, looked like the rock of ages with all that rock's historic accretions still evident. Yet that was just what he was, Cherry thought. The rock of ages. The eternal friend who had goodness next door to his heart and knew the answers to anything that man could do with his two hands, and limitless willingness to help.

" When we've got through," he was saying to Stephen, " we'll lap up a billy a' two of tea and we'll tie them two nags on the back and we'll get back to old Pannikins the drover as soon as the nags 'ull let us. Second thoughts can go one better. We'll tie their reins to their stirrups and give 'em a whack behind. They'll catch up with the old bloke of their own accord. Sooner than later, 'cause they'll go after water."

All the time he was talking he was juggling with the radio and getting a discordance of statics.

" Then we'll pick up them other two," he went on. " Man and a girl, you say? An' we'll shoot through to Timor Bay. Tell you what, feller. I never been in a town since I was a kid. 'Bout time I went to Timor Bay. 'S only four hundred miles on. Could do it by mornin' in this bus."

" We've got a child with us," Stephen said with caution.

" Safe as a homestead in this bus. 'Sides I got plenty of tucker for him. Old Pannikins 'ull have more. How's he go on steaks?"

" Reared to them by this time," said Stephen with a grin.

The air seemed suddenly to clear and Alex Kunder was talking to his brother.

" You wouldn't believe it but they're all alive," he said joyously. " Yep, yep . . . you git through to Timor Bay. See as how you kin git them stations farther south an' west.

Maybe they'll git word through to Yulinga before they do from Timor. Got it? Well look, boy. You'll never guess. I'm goin' to drive 'em to town. Yes, me own true self. An' I don't know what a town looks like——"

Stephen got out of the car and came towards Cherry. She was standing up by the fire. Peter was still sound asleep in the shade of the scrub trees.

Stephen spread his hands in a gesture of finality.

"Well," he said. "It's all over, bar getting to Timor Bay. Hugh and Betty, your people – they'll all know within half an hour."

"And Alan's people too," said Cherry quickly. "He's been worrying about them."

"Of course."

Stephen sat down on his heels, bushman fashion, and lifted the billy from the fire with the help of a short thick stick.

"What sort of people is Alan worrying about, do you know, Cherry?" He was thinking of Alan's general love for the ladies.

She shook her head.

"I wondered. He never said anything very much. Has he got a girl friend do you suppose, Stephen?"

Stephen lifted his head and looked at Cherry.

"Don't you know that?" he asked.

"No. He didn't talk about *one*. Only lots."

Stephen gazed thoughtfully into the fire. Cherry too was sitting down now. She wrapped her arms round her knees and contemplated the flames of the fire.

"It's silly, I know," she said. "But I feel half sad as well as half glad, now that it's all over."

"Thinking about the jungle camp again?"

"Yes. And about everybody who was in it too. Now we each and all go back to the people we belong to. For a little while we belonged only to one another."

"Call it a flash in the pan, Cherry," Stephen said. "It's over now, and finished. If Alan's got a special girl friend somewhere then it's the right thing for him to go back to her. If not . . . why, then I don't think he'll walk right out of your life as if nothing had ever happened. He's not that kind. On short acquaintance I imagine he's a man of honour."

It dawned on Cherry that Stephen had put all her nostalgia for the camp down to some special feeling she might have for Alan Donnelly. She was so surprised she said nothing for a few minutes.

"But then haven't I got some special feeling for Alan?" she asked herself.

Her mind went back to their companionship, his many little acts of kindness. She sat in silence dreamily thinking of Alan Donnelly and all the good things about him.

"You know," she said softly, at length, "I think I was very lucky to be plane-wrecked with the people I was plane-wrecked with. And not least of them Alan. All the same, as I said before, the only boy friend I've got, that I know of, is young Peter. I think I'll have to go back home when this little jaunt is over, Stephen. I'm afraid I'm getting too fond of Peter. Sooner or later that is heart-break for some-one. Me, Peter or Betty."

"If you stayed on the station permanently," Stephen said carefully, "it wouldn't matter how fond you became of Peter. Or he of you."

Cherry jumped up.

"You know I can't do that."

Stephen stood up. He stood beside her, looking down at her.

"You can mend a cracked heart on Yulinga as well as anywhere else," he said. "I think, however, you might find that Alan has ideas of his own."

Cherry was furious now. How dared he keep referring to Alan that way? Couldn't he see it wasn't like that at all? It was other things, other people. She couldn't tell him there was himself, Tracy, even Hugh and Betty Denton to make life complicated for her if she stayed too long on Yulinga. Besides, there was always her duty to go home some time or other.

As Dad had said — some day he and Mummy would grow old. They had no other children. They had taken her,

Cherry, a penniless orphan, and they had made her their own. They had given her everything a father and mother could possibly give to a well-loved child. There was only one way to repay them. She must be on hand against that time when they would need her as badly as she, a baby, had needed them. Duty was a cold word but in this case it had gathered something of warmth to it. There was a call in those singing pines down there by the ocean shore and it wasn't only the call of duty. There was a music in the treetops when the wind blew in them.

The easiest way of going was to let Stephen think what he thought. In that way she would not sound a self-sacrificing prig. It had been priggishness he had laughed at that day he had come to the house in the Street of the Pines.

"Please don't say anything to Alan," she said. "Promise me. You would embarrass him horribly. Me too. In any event I am going back to the Street of the Pines. I promised, and I'll keep that promise."

"Cherry, you were very inexperienced before you came up here. Don't go back to someone you don't really love. Forgive me giving you advice on the subject, but I've nearly fallen into that error myself but grown out of it——"

"Please don't talk about it any more. Oh, here comes Mr. Kunder. Let's have our tea now, then I'll wake Peter." She smiled up at Stephen. "In ten minutes we'll be on our way."

Stephen turned away to ask Alex Kunder what news he had gleaned from his radio talks.

A quarter of an hour later the horses had been dispatched to find their own way to the droving camp, Cherry and Peter were packed in the back of the overlander and Stephen was seated in the front with the station owner. The brake was off, the gears were shifted and the clutch let go. The car rolled forward, the engine contacted and they gathered speed over the floor of the cattle track that led first to the drover's camp at Mulga's End and then on, four hundred miles, to Timor Bay.

At Mulga's End the party was received with whoops

of joy from Alan Donnelly, and the first real spontaneou
smile Cherry had ever seen Tracy wear. Alan and Trac
were mooching round the advance camp waiting for th
rest of the drover's plant to arrive, and for the sight an
sound of bullocks at sundown.

Alex Kunder had made a wide circle of the mob s
as not to rush them but old Pannikins the drover had sighte
the car's dust cloud and not being able to spare his stock
man had sent Stopper the blue heeler to find out what wer
on.

Truly, Cherry thought, that dog had as much understand
ing as a human being. He raced along beside the car an
when nipping at its rear tyres did nothing to attract atten
tion to himself, passed the car, wheeled round and mad
running charges at the front left-hand tyre.

Everyone saw Stopper at the same time. There were crie
of recognition and the car was pulled up. Since Alex Kunde
did not read and write and since neither Cherry nor Stephe
was carrying writing materials, they dispensed with the usua
form of sending a note. A knife was brought out and a loc
of Cherry's hair tied to Stopper's collar.

"That's from you," said Alex.

Stephen gave up his belt and Kunder put the empty packe
of his cigarette papers in the dog's mouth.

"That's from the lot. The kid goes without saying,"
said Kunder. "That'll tell old Pannikins I've picked up th
lot. All right, Stopper old fellow, get to it. Home, boy!"

The dog shot off, a blue streak across the plain, straigh
as an arrow for his master on the eastern flank of the bullock
mob.

Alex Kunder revved up his car again, they gathere
speed and went on to pick up Tracy and Alan at Mulga':
End.

Cherry thought that long car journey to Timor Bay would
never end.

Now that the news was through to the authorities tha
the plane's passengers and pilot were safe there was no
real urgency in getting to journey's end but somehow no

ne wanted to camp again. Any other kind of night camp would be an anticlimax. The adventure was over already and everyone wanted to go home. Kunder himself, having made up his mind he was going to change his way of life and visit a town, couldn't get there quick enough.

Through the night there were periodic stops for refreshment – particularly for Peter – and to change places in the car.

Stephen and Tracy had ridden in the front with the driver for a hundred miles. After that Stephen took over the wheel of the car while Alex Kunder had a nap in the corner back seat. Cherry occupied the other corner with Peter sleeping in a box from the drover's camp lined with some sacks and an old bush rug at her feet. For a long part of the journey Alan sat in the seat between.

There was little said for everyone was partly excited and partly tired. Cherry dozed on and off all the way. She was terribly tired now. That horse ride, though it had not encompassed so many miles, had taken its toll of her. She was stiff everywhere. Small scratches and skin punctures she had from her adventures in the jungle began to make themselves felt. Her one-time injured ankle ached.

Worse, for some unexplained reason, her heart ached too. She felt greatly comforted by Alan sitting silent beside her. What were his thoughts? And was his heart sore too?

How absurd! She must turn over on to her other side and go to sleep again. Thank heaven Peter was such a wonderful sleeper. Each time they stopped he had to be roused to be fed.

"Perfect child," Cherry mumbled to herself, dazed with tiredness. "He's too good to be true."

Perhaps that was why her heart was aching. Peter would no longer be solely hers.

Twice in the early hours of the morning they stopped and changed drivers but Cherry, half asleep, shook her head to proffered refreshment. She would rather sleep, and sleeping forget that to-morrow she would give Peter up. She was sure it was losing Peter that was acting as a weight on her heart.

Stiff and sore she turned round to her left side again and borrowed a shoulder to lean on.

It didn't matter whose shoulder it was, it was a shoulder. That is to say, it gave security and comfort. She turned her face into someone's warm neck and slept.

At daybreak she woke to find it was Stephen's shoulder. He was sitting in the centre seat, one arm round her, his head resting on her head. Long since, it had become Alan's turn to take the driver's wheel. Tracy was still in the front seat, asleep on *his* shoulder. Alex Kunder dozed in the far corner beyond Stephen.

"Oh, I'm sorry," Cherry said, opening her eyes and straightening up, trying not to show the effort was painful.

Stephen opened his eyes. They, too, were hazy with tiredness. He had driven far into the small hours of the morning. The only muscles on his face that moved were those round his mouth. It was that old half-smile, amused but this time kindly.

"Don't be sorry," he said quietly. "I liked it."

"As long as you were comfortable——" Cherry explained.

"I was."

Again they had to change places and it was Stephen who drove them triumphantly into Timor Bay. Alex Kunder, never having been in a town since childhood, didn't understand about negotiating cross-roads and corners.

On the outskirts of the town were a dozen cars and local policeman. Tired and white-faced though they all were, they were escorted triumphantly by the jubilant citizenry to the Road Board office on the northern ocean beach.

After that all was chaos.

People were milling around, officials from the airline company were wringing Alan Donnelly's hand. It seemed that it was a unique feat for him to land a plane the way he did, pancake land on treetops, especially after it had been struck out of action by a bolt of lightning. Furthermore, they felt reassured that as the plane had not gone up in fire they would be able to salvage it. How modest he had been, Cherry thought, a little dewy-eyed. He must have known it had been a wonderful "land."

Reporters asked questions, lights flashed as photographs were taken and delightedly the centre-piece of them all was Alex Kunder, the man who had never been to town before and was now hailed as the rescuer.

Somehow, out of this mêlée Tracy and Cherry were rescued by the wife of the resident magistrate and they were taken home and put to bed.

Cherry would not part with Peter and he had to go home with her and be put to bed in a basket in her room.

Cherry was too tired to notice anything except it was broad daylight, Peter was bathed, fed, played with and put to bed again; the local doctor put coloured paint on all the scratches on all the limbs of the entire party, gave Cherry and Tracy a pill each to swallow and said the girls were not to be disturbed for the rest of the day.

Her bed was beautiful with a foam-rubber mattress and Cherry, after a gloriously soaking hot bath, another cup of tea and a last glance at Peter, sank thankfully on to it.

The only thing wrong was that the party was now divided. They had had to stay in pairs, back there in the jungle. One man and one girl. Now authority, kind friends and civilisation, had parted them.

They weren't together any more – five against the world. Maybe that was why she felt sad when her head went down on that foam-rubber pillow on that foam-rubber bed and someone came in and pulled chintz curtains over the open shutters of the tropical house.

She was in strange pyjamas and someone had put a sheet over her. After that the doctor's pill did its work and Cherry went to sleep.

During the afternoon Cherry's kindly hostess, the magistrate's wife, brought in a bowl of water with scented soap, a soft flannel and towel, and sponged Cherry's face and hands for her.

" But I'm not sick . . ." said Cherry.

" No, but you will be if you don't rest now. You won't get a chance to rest once everyone gets here to welcome you."

" Everyone?"

" Yes, the world and his wife will want to see you. For

173

five days the whole Australian public has thought you a
dead. Your pilot turns out to be quite a hero for pancak
landing a plane on the top of trees and achieving the su:
vival of his passengers – as well as the plane."

"Do they really?" exclaimed Cherry. "Oh, I'm so thank
ful. He was so modest. And so full of concern for hi
responsibility." Her eyes were like stars.

"And the other man too. Stephen Denton from Yuling
Station. He led you out of the jungle. That was a fea:
Most people never get heard of again once they get in there.

"Everyone was wonderful," said Cherry.

"So I've heard. Now I'm going to bring you some te:
and then you go off to sleep again. Round about sundown
there might be a pleasant surprise for you."

"For me?"

"I'm not telling. Now do as you're told. Tea and
another sleep. My daughter's got Peter and he's perfectl
safe and happy."

Cherry had really had all the sleep she needed but th
hot soporific atmosphere worked its chemistry on her. She
dozed on and off, too lethargic to get up, for the rest o
the afternoon.

It was shortly after sundown when the harsh light ha:
gone out of the sky and grey shadows were stealing ir
through the shutters across the room that she heard th
sound of a car coming up the drive of the house. Presently
there was a banging of car doors, men's voices, other voices
strangely familiar, heavy steps on the veranda and yes –
Stephen's laugh.

Her heart gave a painful lurch. She put the back of he:
arm across her eyes for now she *knew*. She really *knew*. She
had known all the time but would never accept it. I:
had taken the sound of his laugh outside the door of a
strange house in a strange town to force her to admit she
was not only in love with him, she loved him. They were
two different complaints and she had them both.

Down there on the beach at the foot of the Street of
the Pines she had fallen in love with him without even

174

knowing his name or even having spoken a word to him. That was something that might have been cured by absence and the process of growing up. But fortune had willed she would go and live in the same house with him, get plane-wrecked in a jungle with him, and find out he was as lovable as he was attractive. To someone like Cherry, young, ardent and wide open to fall in love with a handsome man at fifty yards distance, Fate had played a further hand in the game and dealt out the Jack of Hearts in the middle of a jungle.

Of course he was lovable. Every time he had smiled or teased her she had deliberately turned it into something less kindly.

Why?

Because she had unconsciously been trying to protect herself.

To find him lovable was to love him and to love him was to get hurt. Badly. She was only the governess, and on that station he was a kind of royalty. He belonged to people like Hugh and Betty Denton and Tracy. He belonged to Peter and Peter belonged to him.

There was a dry, unuttered, desolate sob in Cherry's throat.

"They all belong to one another. And I belong to no one. Not even Mummy and Dad."

Cherry pulled herself up with a jerk at this thought.

No, no! She must never allow herself to think this. She had hurt Dad that way before. The way to belong to Mummy and Dad was to make them belong to her, as somehow Peter had come to belong to her; because she had looked after him.

People you look after are yours. That was why she belonged, yes, she *did* belong, to Mr. and Mrs. Landin. She would look after them when they needed it, and then they would belong to her . . .

The voices were talking and laughing outside. She heard Peter's squeal of delight. She guessed now who was out there. Hugh and Betty Denton had arrived. Perhaps they had been brought up from Yulinga by plane. They were finding their lost son.

Well, they'd all be happy now and they could all go home together. Stephen and Hugh and Betty and yes, Tracy Tracy belonged too.

In a minute they would go away, and take Peter with them.

Cherry turned her face into the pillow, and put her hand over her ears.

That is why she did not hear the tap on the door.

The door was opened and first one, then several people came into the room. Even Cherry with her head in the pillow was not deaf to such an invasion. She turned her head and looked across the room. The wife of the resident magistrate was just disappearing behind a whole huddle of people and that huddle consisted of Hugh Denton carrying Peter, and Betty Denton beside him. Standing inside the doorway leaning against the jamb was Stephen. He stayed there as his brother and Betty walked across the room to the bedside. Cherry wiped her eyes on the corner of the sheet because she couldn't find her handkerchief.

Betty Denton sank down on the side of the bed, impetuously put her arms round Cherry and kissed her.

"Hallo!" Cherry said weakly when she could speak.

"I just don't know what to say . . ." Betty was stammering.

Over the top of his wife's head Hugh Denton was being generous with one of his rare smiles. It was Peter who said everything that had to be said. He turned in his father's arms, saw Cherry, gave a shriek of delight and held out his arms. There was nothing for Hugh Denton to do but bend over and deliver his son up to Cherry.

She sat up in bed now, her tears forgotten and real excitement making her forget she was in someone else's pink pyjamas and that a moment ago her eyes had been wet.

"We . . . huh . . . we just don't know how to thank you, Cherry," Hugh Denton was saying.

"Me?" said Cherry in surprise. "You have to thank Alan Donnelly. He landed us alive. And Stephen because he knew the jungle and was able to lead us out of it . . ."

Her eyes went beyond Peter in her arms to Stephen

still leaning against the door jamb. He smiled lazily across the distance to her.

"Two men in a jungle are no good with a baby without a woman around," he said.

"You had Tracy," Cherry said, then bit her lip. It wasn't fair to say that, and yet probably Stephen, man-like – had not registered yet that Tracy had been useless where Peter was concerned. On the other hand, Tracy had been useful in the bush. Cherry must make amends.

"Tracy was wonderful," she said earnestly to Betty and Hugh. "When the lightning struck she didn't move a muscle. Just looked bored. And she wasn't afraid of pythons . . ."

Stephen raised himself slowly from his leaning post. He came across the room and stood at the foot of the bed.

"What were you afraid of?" he asked quietly. "I didn't hear you scream anytime."

"I did lots of times," Cherry said with her old spirit. "Every time you took the law into your own hands about Peter's diet; and when you carried him instead of me carrying him. Only I did it silently."

"What were you afraid of? That I'd poison him? Or drop him?"

"No," Cherry thought. "I didn't really. I knew he was taking care."

"I was jealous," she said honestly. "I was as anxious as a hen with one chick."

They all laughed.

"We're going to have a whole week in Timor Bay," Betty Denton said eagerly. "I'm going to have some treatment for my migraine and Peter is pronounced so healthy after his bush-whacking holiday he is to have his injections at once. Then we're all going back to Yulinga. Cherry dear, we don't want you to leave us ever."

Hugh Denton bent over and took Peter back into his arms.

"When you're ready to get up we're all going out to have a celebration dinner. Your hostess here tells me she thinks one of her daughter's dresses will fit you."

Stephen had taken out a cigarette.

" Am I allowed to smoke in a lady's boudoir?" he asked.
Cherry nodded.

Talking about clothes, she wondered how Stephen came
to be so immaculately dressed. Probably Betty Denton had
brought clothes for him.

" Will Tracy have something to wear?" she asked.

" Yes, one of my dresses," said Betty. " She won't be
pleased but it is better than coming in rags."

" Perhaps . . ."

Betty anticipated what Cherry had been going to say.

" Perhaps Tracy could have the frock that was going
to be lent to you, Cherry? Perhaps nothing," she said quite
firmly. " Tracy always gets everything her way. To-night is
your night."

" But not more than Tracy's——"

" Oh, yes it is. You'll see why later."

Betty Denton was on her feet now and she turned to
her husband.

" What time does that plane get in, Hugh?"

" Anytime now," he said.

Another plane coming in. This sounded mysterious.

" Who is it bringing this time?" asked Cherry, puzzled.
" You're all here, aren't you?"

" We're all here," said Betty, then hesitated. She sought
for some excuse to put Cherry's questions off. She brought the
best one out with a flourish.

" Alan Donnelly's girl friend is being flown up from
Adelaide. She comes in on an evening plane. He was
around Timor Bay an hour ago trying to buy a ring."

Betty said this with the delight and relish that all women
feel when they produce a romance like a white rabbit out of
the air.

" Oh!" Cherry said. Involuntarily her eyes went to Stephen
standing at the foot of the bed. She blushed with confusion
when she realised what Stephen was thinking for his eyes
were watching her closely and there was an expression of
concern in them.

" I'm so glad," she added weakly.

178

"Come on, Betty," Hugh said, touching his wife's arm. "We'd better leave Cherry enough time to get up and put on that glamour."

They turned towards the door. Peter waved happily from his father's arms. And Cherry waved back. Stephen did not move.

"May I have another five minutes, Cherry?" he said, then smiled. "I like you best in a pair of slacks with jungle moss for decoration, and a fringe that doesn't quite stay in place. Hang the glamour."

Hugh nodded from the doorway.

"Don't keep her too long, old man."

"I won't," said Stephen without turning round.

He waited until the others had gone out then he walked round to the side of the bed and sat down on it. He shook the ash from his cigarette on to the small plate on the table beside Cherry's bed.

CHAPTER SIXTEEN

Cherry leaned back against the pillows and pulled the sheet up under her chin. She was unaware of it, but all that showed was a slightly unruly cap of dark hair, a pale face with wide, dark blue eyes that were trying to hide their nervousness. If the eyes succeeded her mobile sensitive mouth did not.

"I'm sorry about Alan," Stephen said gently.

"Don't be sorry about him," Cherry said quickly. "The nicest thing I've heard in the last twelve hours is that he is a hero and not a dud, and that now he's going to get married. Maybe he had to turn out to be a hero for his girl friend to find out she really loved him. I hope she's worth it."

"He certainly has a staunch and loyal friend in you," Stephen said, watching her eyes carefully. "It was only a flash in the pan then?"

"What you're trying to tell me is you think Alan and

I had some kind of love affair in that camp. Well, we didn't. We just got to know one another well. And like one another. At least I liked him."

"He liked you. He thought you were the gamest person ever."

"No more than Tracy."

"Let's leave Tracy out of this."

Cherry saw the sudden tightening of his mouth. There it was again, she thought. That clannishness. That sanctity of family ties. And maybe love too.

Perhaps there were going to be two engagements announced to-night. Maybe it had to be a plane-drop to prove to Tracy Stephen was a hero too – like it was a plane-drop to prove to that other girl that Alan was a hero.

"Has Tracy made up her mind what she is going to do with her future?" Cherry asked, stubbornly keeping on with the subject. Anything to get it over, anything to stop Stephen being sorry for her because Alan was a lost cause and she, Cherry, would be the only girl around at that dinner to-night without a boy-friend. With a stab of wry humour she told herself Peter would be in bed by that time.

Stephen flicked his ash into the plate again.

"Oh yes," he said with a smile. His eyes were full of amusement now. "Tracy has always had her mind made up but she hasn't always let others know it. She's won her point now and even Hugh has given his blessing and approval. Hugh with his conservative outlook has been quite a stumbling block. But with the return of Peter he's willing to give Tracy the world and as far as she is concerned all's well that ends well."

"And you?"

Stephen raised his eyebrows.

"Me?" he said. "What else could I want but the best for Tracy, and every chance of happiness?"

"Of course," said Cherry.

If only he would go now, so she could turn her head in her pillow and have one more little cry. At any rate she could at least get up and do her beastly hair. Oh, if only she'd been able to have it trimmed *before* they got lost in the jungle, instead of afterwards.

"Why couldn't we be plane-wrecked on the way home?" her heart wailed to itself. Hair was an awfully important thing in matters of love. Men loved women whose hair was shining and groomed and properly cut, like Tracy's.

"I wanted to say something special to you, Cherry," Stephen said quietly. "I wanted to thank you for your great kindness to Peter and for the wonderful helpmate you were the whole time we were lost."

Cherry closed her eyes.

"Please don't say anything," she said, embarrassed. "I didn't do anything more than look after a little boy I love." She opened her eyes. She added rather sadly, "You know, I don't think women can help doing things for their children. I mean they don't do it on purpose or because they think it's right. They just do it. Instinct, I suppose."

Stephen stubbed out his cigarette.

"I wanted very specially to thank you and I wanted to ask you something else. Don't think I'm intruding, Cherry, but I feel now I have some right to see if there is anything I can do to add to your happiness." He paused. "You mentioned someone down south to whom you had given a promise to return in a year's time. You heard what Hugh and Betty said about your returning to Yulinga. I too want to add my invitation. I would like you to feel Yulinga is your home. Is there any chance of your feeling that promise you made is no longer valid?"

Cherry crawled farther down in the bed. Unconsciously she had drawn the sheet a little higher and nothing showed now but her nose, her blue eyes and her cap of hair. She shook her head.

"I have to go," she said.

Stephen sat silent on the side of the bed a moment. He seemed to be contemplating the toe of his boot.

"If you have any choice in the matter," he said very slowly, and his eyes came away from the toe of his shoe and looked into Cherry's eyes again, "I would like you to consider an alternative proposition."

There was something so serious and intent in his manner that Cherry's eyes widened and she lowered the sheet an inch.

"I would be very honoured if you would consider becoming my wife," he said. Suddenly his face was creased with his smile, which, like his brother Hugh's, was rare. "Then we could all live happily together ever after, including Peter."

Cherry had the most extraordinary reaction to this proposal.

The sheet went down and she sat up.

"Thank you very much, Mr. Denton. When I get married it will be for love. And I appreciate very much your feelings in rewarding me for loving Peter, with Peter's company ever after." *Dear heaven, I sound like a book, or the third speaker in a public debate. And I haven't any feelings. Why haven't I any feelings?*

In truth she was stunned and said anything that came into her head.

And he didn't expect her to accept, of course. But wouldn't he look silly if she did? How would he explain it to Tracy? He knew, of course, she would decline and be happy to accept the offer as a meaningless compliment.

She decided to be very angry with him, but meantime finish off this small-time piece of formal acting with the politeness the occasion offered.

She held out her hand to him, a little high in the air, like a lady of high distinction who thought her hand just might be kissed.

"Thank you very much for your compliment, and I decline, with due regard to the high honour, with regret."

Stephen took her hand, drew it towards him as if he did indeed intend to kiss it, then suddenly jerked it forward so that Cherry was pulled into his arms. He kissed her abruptly on the mouth.

"Little fool," he said. "You've got no one down there in the south who can give you what I can give you. And apart from all that I love you. *You game little brat.*"

He let her go, and she fell back, eyes wide with astonishment, on to the pillows.

He stood up.

"I'm going to find out about this fellow down south," he said. "And if necessary fight a duel."

Cherry had the sheet up under her nose again. Her voice was muffled.

"How?" she asked weakly.

"How find out? Or how fight a duel?"

"Both."

He turned round, went towards the door, then changed his mind and walked back to the bed. He pulled the sheet away from her mouth, leaned over her so that both hands, one on either side of her, rested on the bed. He kissed her again.

"I'll tell you to-night," he said. "After that plane's come in."

He straightened himself and went back to the door.

"Get cracking, Genevieve," he said sternly. "That dinner is at eight. Your hair needs doing, you might care for a bath and somewhere someone's got a dress of sorts that will fit your royal highness."

He went out of the door and shut it behind him.

Cherry lay on the bed and stared at the door.

Was she waking? Was she dreaming?

Who was mad? Herself or Stephen? And what had the plane coming in got to do with pistols or swords?

It was a wonderful dinner.

They had it alfresco in the gardens of the luxury hotel. All around them was the tropical night, heavy with the scents of strange flowers and night-blossoming trees. Above them was the dark brooding bowl of heaven lit brilliantly with stars that outshone the myriad tiny lights around the garden. Out to sea two pearling luggers lay prow to stern, their lights like a line of glow-worms on the horizon. In the patio of the hotel behind them voices laughed, china clinked and recorded music floated faintly on the air.

The borrowed dress, an almond green silk, fitted Cherry

beautifully and so did an extra pair of Betty Denton's shoes that Betty had brought in her hand luggage.

"I'm terribly sorry that in the excitement I forgot to bring any clothes for you and Tracy," she said. Stephen's fine-looking tropical suit and shirt were actually his brother Hugh's.

"Selfish pair, aren't we?" grunted Hugh. "Can't imagine why we didn't think you wouldn't bring your cases with you out of that jungle."

"I brought one thing with me," said Cherry.

She put her black and silver cosmetic case on the table.

"When I left home in the Street of the Pines I meant to get glamorous, and I sort of, well I sort of . . . couldn't part with it."

Everyone laughed. The idea of putting eye-shadow on in the middle of the jungle was truly funny.

That is, to everyone except Tracy. She turned on Cherry with considerable disdain.

"You might have told me you had that," she said. "We were supposed to share everything."

"Like cigarettes, for instance," said Cherry, and smiled so that her pretty teeth caught an edge of silver from the light in a tree nearby. "I did refrain from using it, and you can't say the same of the cigarettes."

The "heart's desire" that Tracy had gained and which Stephen had spoken of in Cherry's room at the Residency had been explained away.

When Hugh and Betty had gone to see Tracy before they called on Cherry in the late afternoon Tracy had held out her hand as Hugh had come in and said:

"I have saved your infant son's life from the perils of the jungle. Namely pythons. I want my reward, please. One thousand pounds so I can go back to London and get on with my dancing."

Hugh who rarely laughed had thrown back his head and laughed loudly.

"Okay, Tracy, you win," he said. "I've been trustee for your money long enough and you'll be twenty-one in two months' time. You can have some of it now."

Betty had said:

" Wouldn't it be much more fun to settle down and marry Stephen, Tracy——"

" I considered it," Tracy had said from the depths of her pillows for she, like Cherry, was still in bed when the Dentons' plane had flown in from Yulinga. " He works too hard. And by the same token so do the rest of you. I'd rather dance."

" I don't suppose he asked you," Betty guessed shrewdly.

" How right can you be!" said Tracy. " Now if you'll just sign a cheque or two as pin money in the meantime, Hugh darling, and then retire to some place else, I'll get up and book my passage."

The occasion had been too joyous for the entire Denton family to do anything but laugh at Tracy and let her have her own way. Alan Donnelly later suggested it was she who had put that hoodoo on the plane. Anything to get before the footlights of Covent Garden.

Stephen was the only one absent at the early stages of that dinner party.

Alan Donnelly's girl turned out to be petite, attractive and starry-eyed about being engaged to a hero-pilot. Alan was nearly smug but not so smug that he forgot to tell Cherry at frequent intervals what a marvellous pal she had been in troubled times.

There was not only an atmosphere of gaiety about that gathering but also one of mysterious anticipation. This last had something to do with Stephen's absence.

Cherry gathered from desultory remarks that he had gone out to meet " that plane." She hadn't yet discovered what " that plane " was nor why its importance. Planes came into Timor Bay from all over Australia. Alan's girl had come in on one from Alice Springs. Whatever his purpose in meeting this one it had not yet been divulged but Cherry had a feeling everyone except herself was in some kind of a secret. There was an atmosphere of conspiracy. She did not try to probe it for she felt that if they had meant her to know they would have told her.

Perhaps there were other unknown Denton relatives arriving. Perhaps it was a surprise in the form of letters or messages from home. That would be it. He'd gone to get the mail so there would be something special for Cherry as well as for everyone else.

Dear Mummy and Dad! How thrilled they would be to know she was safe.

Suddenly Cherry knew she couldn't bear it if there weren't any letters. Would they have had time to write and the mail get here? They would have heard the news yesterday midday when Alex Kunder had radioed from his car when he found them. That was now thirty-two hours ago. Yes, there would have been time if that mystery plane was from the West Coast instead of from Sydney or Adelaide.

Well, she wouldn't ask. She might be disappointed.

They had had hors d'œuvre and Hugh was discussing the wines with the steward when Cherry saw Stephen come out of the hotel entrance and begin to come across the half-lit garden towards them. He had someone with him. Two people, in fact. A man and woman, and he was walking between them. The woman's hand was on his arm as if he was leading her with pride. The man walked with careful dignity on the other side of him. The light was behind them so Cherry couldn't see who they were.

Then suddenly her heart thumped.

Was it? It couldn't be! It *was*!

She half rose in her chair, then sank down again. Then suddenly she stood up, pushed back her chair and ran across the garden.

She was in her mother's arms, then Dad's arms. Then back to her mother again.

She was saying the silliest things but none of them mattered. Mrs. Landin was saying, "There! There!" and her husband was wiping his eyeglasses with immense care.

Stephen stood back in the shadows. Presently he went towards the table, leaving the three of them alone for a few minutes. Later he turned round.

"Come on, Cherry," he said firmly. "Bring my future mother and father-in-law over to meet my relatives."

Cherry was back to earth with a start.

" *Mummy*——" she said imploringly.

" He's told us all about it, dear," Mrs. Landin said. " On he way into town from the plane. And he was telling Dad all about it in the lounge while I had a bath, and changed. Poor Dad, he's hardly had time to dress properly himself. But he doesn't mind because he's so pleased."

" Dad . . ." Cherry began.

" It's made us very happy, Cherry," he said. " Now when his brother and wife come down south for their holiday in the Street of the Pines you and Stephen can come to us."

" And when we get too old and doddery for that," Mrs. Landin said excitedly, " we're to have a small house on the station near you. Of course I've been up here in the north before. That's how I knew about you, darling. And I know how big those stations are. Big enough for a hundred houses."

" Oh, Mummy!" Cherry said desperately. " But he's done all this without telling me."

" I know, dear. You see, he had to find out if you'd given us a promise about coming back at the end of the year. He knew it was someone, and his sister-in-law told him she thought it was Dad. Then, of course, he had to get our permission for you to break the promise. He is so honourable. I've heard it's quite out-dated for young men to ask parents' permission these days, but Stephen is not at all like that. Most correct and punctilious, I would say."

" Dad?"

" Go ahead. I like this Stephen very much. He'd have to measure up pretty big for me to give you up, you know that, don't you, my dear?"

Stephen had left the table. He came up behind Cherry now and slipped his arm along her shoulders.

" The man from down south has given up, Cherry," he said softly.

Stephen stood holding Cherry imprisoned by his arm while the older couple went across the garden to the table.

Hugh Denton had stood up and was performing the introductions. From the distance Stephen and Cherry stood watching. At last Stephen put up his other hand and turned Cherry's face towards him.

"Well?" he said, the old amused laugh in his voice. "You're not going to ruin their pleasure, are you? They'd be terribly disappointed if you turned me down now."

Cherry swallowed to get rid of a strangled feeling in her throat.

"Stephen, don't you want to know if I love you?" she pleaded.

"You do, darling. It began the night you came to Yulinga and has gone on ever since. And will go on for ever more. I'm right, aren't I?"

She nodded her head, half fearful, half madly happy.

"Just call it chemistry," he said, "if you can't say, 'I love you.'"

"Chemistry," said Cherry suddenly.

The ice was broken. With a catch in her throat she went into his arms. He drew her back into the shadow of the trees and kissed her forehead, the tip of her nose and her chin. Then lovingly he kissed her mouth.

"When this party is over," he promised, "I'll bring you back here and tell you some more about how chemistry works."

"Yes, please," said Cherry. "I didn't learn much about it at school."

"I should think not," said Stephen sternly as he took her arm and led her back to the circle at the table.

Hugh Denton saw them coming and was on his feet.

"We've got the champagne poured," he said. "All we're waiting for is the second couple to toast."

Cherry and Stephen were almost pushed down into two chairs beside Alan Donnelly and his fiancée. The glasses were raised and the champagne in them sparkled in the reflected lights from the trees.

As the others drank, Stephen took Cherry's hand and put it in the crook of his arm so that he could hold it pressed against his body. She turned her head and looked at his profile.

"Oh, Stephen!" her heart cried. "I love you. I love you." She was too shy to put it into words just then, but later, when they would be alone together . . .

She looked at Dad, who was smiling at her.

"To my daughter," he said proudly.

THE RIVER IS DOWN. She had crossed her own Rubicon—now she was free to be a different woman, with a new life.

THE ONE WHO KISSES. Had Hal changed, or had he always been selfish and cruel? And how did he measure up to someone like Rick?

THE MAN FROM OUTBACK. Mari was whisked off to Australia to mend a broken heart—but as soon as she met Kane Manners, her heart was in trouble again. . . .

DOWN IN THE FOREST. The tragedy of the fire had reached them all—but, in its embers, Jill sensed that her dreams might come true.

WIFE TO ORDER. Her guardian had treated Carey as a child—and now he told her coldly that she would soon be his wife. . . .

THE MOONSHINER. Joan fled the social whirl for life in the vast Outback. She learned much of the ways of the wild—and then she learned to love. . . .

THE RANGER IN THE HILLS. Was he a myth or a man? Now that he held her in his arms, Kate would discover the truth about the man she had had to trust.

SHINING RIVER. They had loved each other as children, but now that life's hardships had torn them apart, could they ever recapture the sweet past?

SIX FOR HEAVEN. Theodora had four lively sisters—and four men to choose from!

THE GONE-AWAY MAN. Heartbreak tore Lisa as she watched the man she loved turn to another girl.

KINGDOM OF THE HEART. Judith had to share her inherited cattle farm with darkly handsome Andrew, who felt that the Outback was no place for an unmarried woman.

THE LOVING HEART. He hired Elizabeth to pose as his fiancee to evade designing women attracted by his fabulous wealth. But the masquerade backfired. . . .

MASTER OF RANSOME. He married Sara out of need—not out of love. . . .

JOYDAY FOR JODI. Jodi Dean came to Australia in search of her missing brother—and found herself in a three-way fight over the same man.

To order by mail, send 80¢ for each book to Dept. CS, Beagle Books, 36 West 20 Street, New York, NY 10011.